A Table for Three

A Table for Three

Lainey Reese

SAMHAIN
PUBLISHING

Samhain Publishing, Ltd.
577 Mulberry Street, Suite 1520
Macon, GA 31201
www.samhainpublishing.com

A Table for Three
Copyright © 2011 by Lainey Reese
Print ISBN: 978-1-60928-007-9
Digital ISBN: 978-1-60504-987-8

Editing by Bethany Morgan
Cover by Amanda Kelsey

First Samhain Publishing, Ltd. electronic publication: April 2010
First Samhain Publishing, Ltd. print publication: February 2011

Dedication

Mom,

When I was scared of what people would think if I wrote a steamy novel, you encouraged me. You urged me to write what was in my heart and let my imagination fly... When you read this, remember, you asked for it.

Chapter One

"Hey, where to, lady?" Riley looked into the rear view mirror, met the gaze of the cab driver and smiled with the enthusiasm of a kid at Disneyland.

"I don't know," she said. "This is my first night in New York City."

"Okay then." The cabbie smiled back. "Welcome to the best city in the world, little lady. What are ya needin', huh? You want food? I can tell you where to get the best Italian this side of the Atlantic. What about sightseeing? You ain't never seen nothin' 'til you seen Times Square at night."

"Oh wow," Riley said, lightheaded with the possibilities. She thought the balding, unshaven man exactly fit her image of a New York cab driver. "Could you please take me to a night club? I've always wanted to go to one like I've seen in the movies. You know, one that you have to wait in line to get in, and it has movie stars and famous people mixed together with everyday people."

Carl chuckled, "Listen, I know a good place, the best. But you gotta promise me that you won't do nothin' stupid if I take you there." He pulled the cab into traffic as he spoke and flicked a stern look at her in the rear view mirror again. "It's the hottest club in the whole city, packed with a lotta famous folks. But like I said, you gotta be careful. It's got a kinda weird reputation, like it's some kinda Studio 54 or somethin' and that a buncha kinky shit goes on...oops" he stammered and flashed her a grimace. "I mean stuff, kinky stuff goes on. So you play it smart. You don't leave with nobody. You don't let no one but the waiter bring you a drink, and whatever you do, don't drink anything that you've left at the table or somthin' stupid like that. Got it?" He raised a bushy dark brow at Riley and waited for a reply.

"Got it." She smiled at him and wondered where the silly rumors about cab drivers being rude came from if they were anything like this one. "I'll be good."

"No," Carl interrupted, "forget good, you be smart. I ain't kiddin' 'bout this place. You want New York nightlife, this is it in spades. You gettin' all the glitter you could want, but you gotta steer clear of the dark side of it, okay? No getting caught in dark corners or drinkin' too much booze and gettin' drunk. You find a table where you can just sit and watch, you don't gotta mingle too much on your first night." As he made his way through the maze of streets and the snarls of traffic, Riley gazed out her window in awe. "So how long you in town?"

"Oh I'm staying," she replied. "My work transferred me here."

"No kiddin'? Good for you. What kinda work you in?"

"I'm an operation's manager for a bank."

"Huh?"

Riley smiled at him in his rear view mirror, "It's my job to make the schedules and do the audits and order supplies and stuff like that. I've always wanted to live in New York so when a position opened up here, I went for it." Riley flung her arms wide and thought that the work and the wait had been worth it. "And here I am. It seems like a dream. I can hardly believe I'm here."

"Well, good for you," Carl said. "You gonna make it just fine here I can tell." He smiled at her and pulled up in front of the club. "Now, remember what I said. Be smart."

Kincade Marshall was going to kill his bouncer. As the owner of one of the hottest clubs in New York, he thought he could probably get away with it. His bouncer, Gary, was too soft on the women.

"What the hell are you doing?" Cade demanded, standing not two inches from Gary. He motioned to the other man on the door for the night. "Take over for a moment, Tom. Gary is going to take a quick break." With a hand in the middle of Gary's back, Cade led him into the crowded nightclub speaking directly into his ear as they went. "We've been over this. You know the profile we're looking for. So I'll ask you again. What the hell are you doing?"

Cade knew Gary understood, they'd been down this road before—the little brunette didn't fit the bill.

"Cade, man, I know. I know but she's hot. Now, I know she looks kind of sweet, but, I'm keeping an eye on her and I'll make sure she doesn't get into any trouble."

Cade heard the hopeful note in Gary's voice, "I was hoping that she'd hang around until my shift was over."

"Look, this is an exclusive club where our patrons can come without the threat of exposure. The people here come with the knowledge that no matter what they do or who they do it with, it will never leak. There will never be a tell-all book, or an exclusive on Oprah or a tabloid full of hidden snapshots. This club is under the radar and the only people allowed in here are the ones whose lives depend on it staying that way."

Cade's face took on an expression that made Gary take an involuntary step back. "You had to work here two years before I trying not to gawk. She wanted to fit in, not look like the out-of-towner she was. She'd actually felt his stare before she saw him. Slowly, like a scene out of a movie, she looked at the body of the man in front of her.

He was dressed in black and, from the way the shirt clung to his impressive chest and shoulders, it had to be silk. He had a strong neck, a nice jaw and then she noticed his mouth and almost didn't want to look any further. She could definitely picture herself on the receiving end of those lips. She brought her gaze up to see a strong Roman nose saved from being perfect with a bump that let her know he'd broken it and wasn't vain enough to have it fixed.

She met his eyes. It wasn't just that they were blue. It was that they were electric. She didn't think it was the lighting that made them glow—it had to be the intensity with which he stared. Everything in her just seemed to melt. Despite the cab driver's warnings, she knew to the tips of her toes anything this man wanted she would do.

Anything.

Her nipples hardened. She actually felt her body clench and moisten, and he hadn't done more than look at her. In an instant her mood went from playful and adventurous to something she had never felt before but could only name as ravenous.

"I.D.," he said and held out his hand to her.

She didn't question who he was or why he wanted it. She grabbed her license out of her purse and handed it to him. She also didn't stop to think why she would do what he asked. She just knew whatever he asked her for, she would do it.

Cade looked at her for several seconds after she handed him her I.D. before he could tear his gaze away. No wonder

Gary had risked his job to let her in. He watched while her nipples puckered and pushed against the soft fabric of her dress and when she squirmed in her seat, he knew it was because she was getting wet.

Everything in him tightened as he recognized the signs she was as affected by him as he was by her, and it made him feel like an animal. He now understood why wolves marked their territory. The urge he felt to claim her was just as basic and fundamental. He tore his gaze down to the license in his hand and saw that her name was Riley Makenna Ramirez. She was twenty-three, five two and weighed one hundred and fifteen pounds. There was also an out-of-state address.

He looked up and quirked a brow at her. "Washington?"

"Oh, I, uh, just moved here," Riley stammered. "I only got in today, but it's real I swear. I have some other I.D. if you want to see it, a bank card and a credit card too, but those don't have a picture."

Cade would have smiled at her rambling if he wasn't in such a state of arousal. He didn't doubt it was a real license. He just wanted to make sure she wasn't planning to catch a plane any time soon. Not that she'd make that plane but it was a complication he wanted to prepare for.

He handed the card back to her. "No need." He motioned to a server close by and when she hurried over he ordered two drinks. She was getting something a little stronger than diet cola whether she wanted it or not. "May I?" He took the chair next to her as he asked to make it clear her assent was assumed. A not so subtle way of establishing who was in control.

He was a self-aware man. He knew what he liked and how he liked it in every aspect of his life. He made no apologies about his lifestyle and didn't understand or have patience with anyone who did. He was a dominant. He liked raw, earthy sex and he demanded absolute control of his women. He did not take a lover who wasn't open to sharing. He and his best friend Trevor had shared every girlfriend they'd had since their freshman year of college. It wasn't that they didn't both enjoy one-on-one sex. They did. But lovers had to welcome them both.

He didn't talk to her as they waited for the drinks. Another show of dominance. A simple test to see if she would follow his lead. He also made very little eye contact, but watched her out of the corner of his eye to see how she would handle being ignored. At first, she watched him with a bright smile showing straight white teeth and eager eyes. After a moment, her smile dimmed and she looked around to try to see what he was looking at.

Most women would start to fidget and try to break the ice, assuming that he wanted her to make the moves. The ones who paid attention and were on the right wavelength, those women would keep their eyes on him and wait for him to take the lead. Riley was on the right wavelength.

She wasn't a practiced submissive because she didn't lower her eyes and take a slave posture but she did have a submissive streak in her because she was waiting for him. There was spirit in her wait. She had one corner of her mouth curved up in a smirk and a twinkle in her eye that dared him to talk first. She thought this was a game.

Her only mistake was she didn't realize this was a game that was going to change her life forever.

The drinks came and he sent the server away with a whispered message to tell his manager he was to be undisturbed for the remainder of the night. Then he took his magnetic key card out of his pocket and swiped it thru the mechanism in the center of the table that activated the hollow

Plexiglas privacy shield.

The table was under the second floor balcony, away from the dance area with a wall behind them. The shield came up from the floor in a semicircle sealing them against the wall. As soon as it reached the ceiling, the hollow glass filled with a smoky, swirling mist but never filled completely. The smoke allowed shifting glimpses in as well as out. It was a favorite with the voyeurs as well as the exhibitionists.

Riley's whispered, "Wow," made him smile, and he shifted his gaze to her. She looked like she had just seen a magic trick, and her delight was unmistakable.

"Riley," he said, "my name's Cade. I don't think you realize the type of club you've stumbled into. I'm going to make myself perfectly clear." He never broke eye contact as he spoke, picked up her martini, and brought it to her lips to drink. She was staring at him with wide eyes. He had a hard time keeping the smile off his face when she wrinkled her nose at the first sniff of the drink he had ordered her. Her hands fluttered when she tried to take the drink from him and realized he intended to hold it for her while she sipped from his hand. This was supposed to be a serious moment and she was making him smile.

"Tell me something. What do you hate most? Something so bad you can't stand it."

"Spinach," Riley answered quickly. "What about you?" she asked.

"No. No questions now. Just listen."

Spinach? Cade chuckled and shook his head. He had asked dozens of girls that question and heard everything from spiders and snakes to pap smears. This was the first time anyone had picked a food. Damn, it looked like he was going to be going without some of his favorite dishes for the foreseeable

15

future. He liked spinach.

"Okay, spinach," he continued. "That's your word. That's your safety net. From this moment forward, that word is your way out. If something hurts, if something is too much, if in any way this is more than you want or think you can handle, that one word is your way to stop everything. Think about that. Never use that word lightly. Never say it unless you want to walk away and never look back. No matter what is happening or what we're doing that word is your assurance that you have the control."

She slowly stopped sipping as his words went on, and he could see by the look in her eyes she was starting to get an idea of the direction this night was going to go. He didn't see fear, only a serious contemplation of what she was hearing.

"Riley, I want you to understand that will be the only control you have when you are with me." She gulped loud enough for him to hear and squirmed in her seat again. No, she wasn't afraid, she was curious and turned on.

"Take another sip." He hadn't taken the glass from in front of her, but she had stopped drinking. He waited to say anything else until the drink was half gone. Then he heard her mumble with another wrinkle of her nose that she probably should have said alcohol instead. He set the drink down and took her delicate chin in his hand as if he needed to assure that she didn't miss what he had to say next.

"It starts now. Right here, right now. If you do not want to get bent over this table and fucked in this booth, I suggest you say spinach. I'll let you go with the warning to never come back here again unless you're ready for it."

Riley gulped. This could not be happening to her. She was Riley Ramirez. She was a bank manager whose butt was too big. She did not have sexy gorgeous men want to *do* her in a public place. This had to be a dream. A really good dream and she was going to wake up tomorrow and wish stuff like this did happen.

In her wildest fantasies, she wouldn't have thought something like this could happen to her. As she saw it, she had two options. She could say spinach, leave, and in two weeks start her new job. Then for the rest of her life wonder what it would have been like. On the other hand, she could keep quiet and see where this was going to go. Take a leap and do something wild, something daring, and something completely forbidden. Did she have the guts? Did she dare to do what every woman would do if she didn't have to answer for it in the morning, if she only had the gumption? Did she?

Riley took a deep breath.

"Like I said," she whispered, "I hate that stuff, so why would I say it now?"

She expected him to kiss her but he didn't. Instead he stood and moved behind her. She felt his hands on her shoulders and shivered as he squeezed them and moved those strong fingers up her neck and into her hair. He brushed her hair to the side and she felt his warm breath a second before his hot mouth bit lightly into the sensitive skin where her shoulder and neck met.

He swirled his tongue as he sucked hard enough to leave a mark, and Riley couldn't hold back a moan or the shudders that were taking over her body. His hands slid the thin straps of her dress off her shoulders and delved into the front of her gown. Gently, he pulled the material of her dress and bra down until her breasts were exposed and the material was bunched under them, thrusting the mounds up. Riley gulped and thought of what he was seeing. The tips of her breasts were a dusky, rosy brown, and he would see they were already tightly beaded.

Cade's hands were running up and down her arms. She didn't know what to do. She wanted to touch him, and she wanted him to touch her breasts so bad she was ready to beg, but she didn't know how to ask for it. This was far beyond what she knew about sex and foreplay. She was starting to think the two guys she had been with didn't even count. Because Cade hadn't really done anything yet, and already it was the best sex she'd ever had.

"Stand up," Cade said. Riley stood. Cade gave a dark smile at her unquestioning compliance as he moved her chair out of the way. With one hand wrapped around her delicate throat he brought her back to his front and slid his other hand along the outside of her body, grazing breast, waist, hip, thigh. "Fucking perfect. Did you know you were perfect?" The top of her head fit under his chin and he leaned down to whisper in her ear.

"No. I'm too chunky," she croaked, turned on and just scared enough to flavor her arousal without ruining it. "My-m-my butt's too big and my thighs too."

"Sshh." Cade squeezed just a little on her throat and started inching her skirt up. "Never say anything like that again. You're perfect. Women without curves aren't women, they're boys with long hair. You," he growled as her skirt revealed her thighs and hips with a little scrap of red lace at her crotch, "are definitely a woman." He slipped his fingers into the lace at her hip and gave a sharp tug, neatly tearing them from her body. He brought the lace up in front of her face and spoke with his lips on her cheek.

"Nice. I think I'll keep these as a souvenir." He brought the lace closer to their faces, and Riley thought she just might come right then when he took a long sniff. She felt his erection get even bigger against her back.

"Very nice," he said and straightened. His hand around her neck shifted to grip a fistful of hair at the back of her head. He slowly pushed until she was bent over the waist-high table and her bare ass was in the air. The combined sensation of the cold table on her nipples and the hot man at her back brought another moan from her. She thought if he didn't touch something vital soon she'd start begging.

Cade was about to lose control. That wasn't like him. So far this was pretty tame by most standards, especially his, but her scent, her obedience, the way she quivered with need was awakening something dark and primitive in him. He wanted to drag her off like a cave man.

He took a good long look at the ass and thighs she claimed were too big and almost drooled. Her ass was lush and looked like a feast to him. Her thighs were curvy and full, just barely touching under her luscious little pussy. He didn't need to touch that sweet flesh to see if she was ready—it was wet and glistening, begging for a good hard ride. Cade quickly unfastened his slacks and pulled his cock out. He briefly let go of her to fish a condom out of his pocket, open it, roll it on and then reclaim his fistful of hair. "Spread your feet," he said. She did with a whimper. "Wider." She did. He shifted forward and positioned the swollen head of his shaft against her, then grabbed a handful of her lovely hip and shoved inside her hot wet channel.

Riley screamed. It was a scream of passion, of lust and need. It was amazing.

The sound tightened his balls and tested his control even farther. He pulled out and thrust again and again. Each time he thrust, she yelled. Her voice was guttural and raw, not the practiced sounds of a woman who was trying to inflame her lover, but the real sounds of a woman about to lose her fucking mind in an orgasm. His hand tightened in her hair, and he pulled her head back toward him as he leaned over her and shifted so that his cock nestled even further inside her pussy and bumped against her cervix with each thrust.

"Like that do you, Ry?" he whispered, and his tongue came out to delve into her ear. When she did no more than quiver and moan, the hand holding her hip slapped her hard on the ass, and he gave a good tug on her hair. "Answer me. Always."

"Y-Yes," she stammered. "Yes, I like it." He thrust again and she moaned long and loud. "I like it a lot."

"Riley, I want you to come for me," Cade said as he started pumping into her faster and harder, using all his control to keep from coming himself as her tight little pussy clenched around his plunging shaft. Riley's hands started scrabbling on the table, and he heard her say, "Oh God" as her body started to tighten and buck against him.

"Fuck," he muttered as he struggled to hang on and keep her in place. It was like watching a volcano just before it erupted as she drew closer to her peak. "That's it, baby, come, come for me...ugh, don't move...fuck." Her body heaved, and her pussy clenched his dick as hard as a fist. There was no chance of him not coming with her. Her orgasm flooded over him like lava and brought a shout to his own throat as it swamped him. His body started bucking and thrusting into her while hot jets of come shot out of him. She continued to moan and thrash within the small bit of room he allowed her until the worst of the storm had passed.

With his vision a little fuzzy at the edges and his cock already stirring up for another round, Cade pulled out of her and righted his clothes. He'd wait until later to remove the condom since there was nowhere to dispose of it here. He smiled at the way she stayed spread across the table exactly as he left her, her eyes closed and a smile trembled on her lips.

He smoothed her skirt down over her ass and gave it an affectionate squeeze before he retrieved his chair and sat close to her side with his legs bracketing hers. She was still keeping her eyes closed and had one dainty hand curled up under her chin, showcasing the lovely curl of her back and shoulder. Her hair was a cascading waterfall of chocolate over her and the table.

Cade was content to let her linger for the moment. He picked up his drink and took a few swallows. His hand went back to her ass—he didn't think he'd be able to keep his hands off it for very long. With a sigh he pulled her closer into the vee of his legs. He used the icy bottom of his glass to slide some hair away from her cheek and was charmed when she shivered and goose bumps spread across her shoulder.

"Open your eyes, Riley."

"Okay," she said as she did, "but I don't think I can see yet."

He chuckled. Her pupils were dilated and unfocused, the dark brown irises looking like melted chocolate. She blinked at him slow and sweet, and his heart tripped with a pleasant dose of affection to go along with the lust he felt for her.

"I've never done anything like this before," she whispered as if she was afraid someone would hear *that* but not the ear-piercing screams she'd been making.

"I know." He chuckled as he took another drink. "I'm glad you liked it. It's only the beginning."

"I was hoping you'd say that."

"Good, fix your dress, I'm going to open the shield and take you to my penthouse where we can do this properly."

She stretched like a kitten after a nap with her hands sweeping up through her hair and then out as far as she could reach in front of her while she arched her back. It bowed her body in a curve over the table, and her full breasts swayed with the movement. She slowly straightened and used her hands to push herself into an upright position.

If she had been trying to tempt him she would have stretched after she stood so she could shake her amazing breasts at him, but the way that she'd done it was all the more alluring for its lack of artifice. She moved like a woman who'd been deliciously fucked and couldn't be happier about it. With a few tugs, a wiggle and a dainty bounce she had her dress back in order. He'd kept her snug against his crotch the whole time so she couldn't miss the fact that he was hard again and wanting more of her. He reached out and gave a tug on the dress to bring it down enough to show a hint of the lacy red bra she wore before he pressed the button that opened the shield.

He stood, took her hand and walked toward the bar on the other side of the club. Riley looked around for someone pointing or laughing or something, but no one seemed to care what they had been doing. Riley released the breath she didn't know she had been holding. She saw they were heading away from the front door.

"Um, Cade." She had to shout to be heard above the music and crowd. She knew he heard but he didn't stop. She shouted louder. He finally stopped and turned to face her with an eyebrow quirked in question.

"I thought we were going to your place," she said and pointed to the door. Cade gave her a look and tugged back on her hand and continued the way he'd been going. Oh well, Riley thought, maybe they were getting a drink first. Then her mouth dropped open when he led her around the bar to a shiny black elevator that opened with the same card he'd used to activate the privacy shield.

Cade pulled her in behind him, and as soon as the doors slid closed, it started its ascent. He leaned back against the wall and pulled on her hand to bring her against his chest. He gently cupped her face in his palm and leaned down until his forehead rested against hers and their breaths mingled nicely. Riley sighed and let her body drift and loosen 'til she was draped against him from the ankles up. She looped her loose arm around his neck with a smile and a sigh. "This is nice," she whispered against his lips. "Now can I ask a question?"

He smiled back. "Yes, you may."

"Are you ever going to kiss me?"

"I am going to kiss every inch of you, including that luscious mouth of yours, but not yet. You have to wait."

"Wait for what?"

"This," he said, and the elevator doors slid open.

Chapter Two

She was in a high-rise penthouse—it wasn't a dream, it was heaven. Maybe her plane had crashed and this was how she was going spend eternity. Riley stumbled forward to the middle of the room and turned in a slow circle as she tried to take in everything. Cade's whispered, "Look around while I clean myself up," barely registered.

It was impossible. It was glass and chrome and big windows with a postcard view. It was decorated mostly in black with bold splashes of jewel tones to pop in all the right places. There was an amazing piece of glass artwork in swirling shades of reds and golds on the mantel. There were matching black leather couches in front of the fireplace with throw pillows in emerald, sapphire and blood red ruby. She could see a dining area with an ebony table that shone like glass on an area rug, which looked like it must have cost a fortune. There was tasteful artwork on the walls giving the place the feeling of a high-class art gallery.

She could not believe this was actually happening. She moved like a sleepwalker to stand in front of the floor to ceiling windows and almost wept at the sparkling view of the city laid out before her.

"Breathtaking," she whispered in awe just before Cade's arms came around her and she found out what having her breath taken away was really like. He scooped one big hand against the back of her head and his other arm banded like steel around her back. Then at last he kissed her. His kiss was as devastating as his lovemaking had been. He kissed with his whole mouth—tongue, teeth, lips and the effect was making her head spin. His tongue filled her mouth, and his hand shifted the angle of her head so he could get in even further. His tongue thrust in and out. Riley started to quake, she could not call this kissing, he was making love to her mouth with his and she had never felt anything more glorious.

Cade's arms grew tighter and tighter as the kiss went on, and his moans rose to match hers. Within minutes, their hips were mimicking the motions of their mouths.

Cade shoved her against the window. He brought both his hands to the sides of her face then slid them down, over her neck and shoulders and finally to her heaving breasts. Both hands squeezed the full mounds, Riley groaned in ecstasy around his kiss and her hands started clutching his shirt trying to get under the silk to his skin. Cade grabbed material on either side of her chest and gave a sharp yank, breaking the dainty straps and baring her luscious breasts to him. With a growl, he tore his mouth from hers and latched onto her nipple with hungry lips while her other one was engulfed in the heat of his palm and fingers. He fed at her breasts, alternating from one to the other, sucking, biting, lapping and squeezing while Riley moaned and thrashed against the window.

It wasn't enough. He needed more. He let go of her breasts to reach behind her to the zipper in the back of her dress and roughly yanked the offending material away along with the strapless bra she wore. He thanked God for her bare legs as he smoothed his hands up her thighs to the wet heat between them. His teeth nipped hard on a nipple at the exact moment he

25

shoved two fingers deep inside her wet sheath. Something dark and primitive glowed inside him when she screamed and came right then.

Her cunt pulsed around his fingers as he continued to pump into her and then dropped to his knees and used his tongue on her. Her scent and taste was a smoky, musky tang with a heady mix of the fruity perfume she'd used—an intoxicating brew that made it hard for him to resist biting too deep and hurting her. His mouth licked and sucked and tugged at her swollen sensitive clit while he added a twist to the fingers he was fucking her with. He felt another orgasm boiling in her. "That's it," he growled against her sweet flesh. "That's it. Give it to me. One more. Ahhh, yeah." Her knees buckled and her hips pistoned against him as she flew apart again He thought he was going to lose his fucking mind.

He stood and kissed her full and hard, filling her senses with the taste of her own juices. He ripped his pants open, then his hands went to Riley's shoulders and he pushed her to her knees. She looked up at him with big wide eyes as if she didn't know what to do.

There was a red fog of lust clouding his vision, and he had to take a deep breath to fight it back long enough to ask, "Haven't you done this before?"

Riley's eyes were solemn as she shook her head no. She was afraid it would disappoint him, but instead it brought a grim smile of satisfaction to his mouth and his hand to the back of her head.

"Open your mouth." As soon as she did, the swollen, bulbous head of his cock slid in. It was salty and smooth, and there was a dark flavor to him that made everything inside her clench in response. It tasted earthy and primal and it uncaged something inside Riley that she hadn't known was in her. She closed her lips around the head and licked at it the way he had licked at her. His hand tightened and jerked in her hair, and his shaft became bigger in her mouth.

"Mmm. That's it," he said as he started a slow slide in and out between her lips. "Just like that. Ahh yeah, more tongue. Mmm, suck harder." His dark words thrilled her as much as having him in her mouth did. She'd had friends talk about giving head, but she'd never been inclined to do this with the guys she'd been with.

Cade knew he was the first to breach those sweet lips, and it was enough to make him crow like a maniac. She caught on quickly, and her hands started to caress and explore his ass and legs. God, she was a sensual creature. How had she stayed so sheltered and untouched? Weren't there men in Washington? He didn't care how. He was only thankful that he'd been the one to find her, and the last coherent thought he had was he just might give Gary a raise. He tightened his fist even more in her hair and said, "Open your mouth wider."

She did and he shoved in 'til he was lodged against the back of her throat. At first, she started to struggle and back away. "Hold still and relax your throat. Slide your tongue out along the shaft, that'll keep it from gagging you. There you go. That's good. That's right. It won't choke you, just breathe through your nose."

She slowly relaxed and soon the tension eased out of her, and she swallowed around him. "Ahh, do that again."

She did.

"That's so fucking good, baby," he said and started thrusting into her. He knew it was rough, but it was the way he liked it and it would be best if she learned what he liked from

impressed look and continued while he fed her a cube of mild white cheddar. "I'm thirty-four, healthy and I come from a good family. Now your turn. Tell me what brought your lovely little ass to my club."

Riley smiled and picked a cube of cheese to feed him before starting. It took her a second because his teeth nipped at her finger when he took it. "Um, I, well... I was born in Washington. I've never been anywhere, not even Disneyland. We weren't what you'd call rich, not really poor; I mean we did all right. But there wasn't enough money for travel or college."

Cade didn't comment just continued watching her and chewing. He'd bet anything she would have loved a chance at college, it showed on her face and in the way she started to fidget.

"Well. New York. Hmm. I've always dreamed of coming here. But to be honest, this is so far beyond any dream I ever had." Here she stopped with a wistful sigh before continuing. "Well, I didn't have any money saved up," She wrinkled her nose at him, "I am terrible with money. I spend every penny I get. My mom and dad had to take my checkbook from me 'cause I kept overdrawing my account. Don't say anything. Pitiable I know. But there it is. The first step to correcting a character flaw is admitting you have one right?"

"Right." He laughed.

"Right, so, since I was so bad with money I was still living at home. I decided that if I was going to get here, I'd have to work for it. So I got a job at a bank as a teller and started saving and working my way up. It was hard at first, but before long my savings was growing, and I was getting promotions. I found out that after two years I would be eligible to transfer to any branch in any state I wanted. So I waited and kept saving. After my two years was up I applied for the first position that opened here and miracle of miracles I got the job."

"My plane got in at two this afternoon and after I unpacked I dressed up and called a cab that brought me here," she finished with a smile and sent him a look that heated his blood and had his shaft growing again. "You know, I really wish I had tipped that cabbie more." She smiled and leaned forward to kiss him.

Cade chuckled and gripped her chin to keep her close for a deeper kiss. He moved the tray to the bedside table and pulled her to his side. With a few tugs and shifts they had the blankets over them and despite her best efforts, her eyelids started to droop.

"Normally I would scold you for not taking the time to rest, but I have to admit I'm glad you didn't. It's after three in the morning. Get some sleep and we'll talk later. We have a lot to go over."

Chapter Three

Three and a half hours later the sound of the elevator had Cade shifting and opening his eyes. Trevor walked in with eagerness in his long stride. He didn't stop until he was at Riley's side of the bed. Without waking her, Cade smoothed her hair away from her face and gently turned her so Trevor could see her clearly. His indrawn breath and soft whistle was just what Cade expected.

"Beautiful," Trevor whispered. "Perfect."

Cade gave him a look that said he hadn't seen anything yet and lifted the blankets away from her body. "Holy shit," Trevor breathed and tore his gaze away from her body to Cade with an expression on his face that reminded him of a kid at Christmas. The look they shared was one forged over long years of building something deeper and warmer than a friendship. It was a look that said they both knew what was going to happen and words were unnecessary.

"Sweetheart," Cade began, kissing her cheek and gently shaking her shoulder. "Wake up. There's someone here I want you to meet." Trevor squatted at the side of the bed so when her eyes opened she'd be able to see his face.

"C'mon on, sleepyhead, let Trev see those gorgeous eyes of yours."

Riley stretched and sighed, not ready to give up yet on

sleep. Then Cade's words sank in, and her eyes flew open in shock while her whole body jolted. Sure enough, there was someone in the room with them. Moreover, it was a man.

"Shhh," Cade soothed. "It's okay. This is my best friend, Trevor Wellington." Cade turned her face until she looked at him so she would not mistake what he said next. "You are going to obey him the way you do me."

Cade watched her to make sure this wasn't going to have her screaming spinach. He'd let her go if she did, nothing about this worked without her trust, but he was going to do everything he could to make sure she didn't. Her mouth started opening and shutting like a landed fish, and Cade kissed her, thrusting his tongue deep and using all the skill he had at his disposal to light enough fires in her to keep her open to the possibilities in front of her. It worked. Her legs started to slide against his and a soft moan purred up from her throat. He broke the kiss and with his chin motioned toward Trevor. "Say hello to Trevor."

Fear and trepidation came back in her eyes. It wasn't the panic that it had been at first, now it was manageable. "It's all right. Nothing is going to happen to you that you can't stop with one word. All I'm asking is for you to say hi and see what happens from there."

Riley slowly looked at Trevor, who watched every move they made with an intense stare. When her gaze met his, he smiled and said, "Hi. Nice to meet you." His chin rested on the mattress mere inches from her face, and she felt his breath feather across her lips seconds before he moved and kissed her. His kiss was different from Cade's, his lips not as full but just as potent. Where Cade's kiss was thrust and plunge, Trevor's kiss was soft biting nips and brief tingling strokes of his tongue. She purred into his mouth and followed his lead, nipping and stroking back. He brought one hand up to brush her hair from her face, slipped it under the covers to close over her right breast, then he slid onto the bed with them.

Riley stopped trying to think, or reason, or question what was right or wrong. She believed Cade, she didn't know how or why, but she truly believed that she would be able to walk away at any time. If she wanted to. Right now, right or wrong, walking away was the last thing she wanted to do.

Trevor's grip and kiss quickly went from light and teasing to serious. His hand tugged and pulled at her nipples with a strong grip while his tongue, teeth and lips kissed her like she'd never been kissed before. Cade pulled the covers away and slid his hand up her thigh before gripping her knee and draping her leg over his hip.

Her first instinct was to pull her legs closed and cover that part of herself from being so exposed, but both men simultaneously reacted. Cade's teeth bit into her shoulder and Trevor pulled on her nipple, hard. Trevor's eyes opened and stared straight into hers as he slowly slid his hand down her body to her waiting, exposed flesh. His lips brushed against hers with every word, as he said, "You don't make one move without our permission and you'll never have our permission to keep this from us."

His fingers combed thru the soft, sex-dampened hair, over the swollen lips, and then delved deep into her hot, wet channel. A cry broke from her throat and her back arched against Cade. Her hips started to sway and thrust of their own accord, and it became impossible to keep quiet or still, no matter that she was supposed to try. Cade growled behind her, hooked an arm under her knee and lifted her leg high to give Trevor even better access. Trevor took advantage of it. He changed his angle, added another finger and started rubbing her clit with his thumb.

"Damn," he said, speaking to Cade without taking his gaze from her thrashing and twisting body. "She's so hot and tight. That's it, sugar, that's it. Fuck my hand. Come for us, Riley, let me see what you look like when you come." He pumped faster into her, made sure that his thumb never left her clit and with a low guttural cry she came, her body bucking and twisting in Cade's vise-like grip.

Trevor could not believe how responsive she was, and her sweet little pussy was pulsing on his fingers as if it was trying to milk them. The sweet perfume of her orgasm was making him lightheaded. "Fuck yeah. Cade, we are going to have to get rid of this though," he said and tugged on a lock of her pubic hair. He looked at Riley's face and sent her a mischievous wink. "We don't like anything interfering with our meals when we eat out."

"Don't mind him, baby." Cade's voice was filled with warm affection as he spoke in her ear. "He's a smart ass who thinks he's clever." He nuzzled her cheek and ear as he continued, "But he's right about that hair. We want you as smooth and silky on the outside as you are on the inside."

"Cade, care to do the honors?" Trevor asked as he shifted to bring his face in line with her pussy.

"My pleasure," Cade replied and slid her leg back over his hips. Then his hand made a bold firm stroke over her mound and his fingers spread her lips wide, leaving her clit exposed. He shifted his body until his shaft was nestled between the luscious globes of her ass and held her in place while he started sliding between the supple cheeks. Trevor's fingers returned to her tight channel as his mouth descended to the throbbing nub that Cade presented like an offering for him. Cade's other arm was under Riley's head, and he turned her face for a kiss that filled her mouth with a thrusting rhythm that matched the slide of his cock along the cleft of her ass.

Riley couldn't think. This was overwhelming and overpowering. There were two men making love to her. Two. This couldn't be her. But as her body was swamped with sensations she couldn't name and couldn't contain, she stopped trying to think. She couldn't hold still and had to do something, so she reached one hand to Trevor's wavy brown hair and the other to Cade's black then fisted on both and pulled as another orgasm started boiling up from the center of her body.

Just when Trevor sensed she was close again, he curved his fingers up with a twist to thrust against her g-spot. She screamed and jerked causing his teeth to bite into her delicate flesh too hard before he could pull back. "Dammit," he cursed at her yelp of pain. Cade and Trevor both reacted. Cade's grip tightened painfully and his teeth clamped on her tongue holding her frozen. Trevor sat back and gave a sharp slap right on her clit. While Cade's glare blazed into her shocked eyes, she heard Trevor speak with a rumbling growl in his voice and a stinging slap to her clit with each word. "You. Don't. Move. Unless. You're. Told." Riley squeaked and shook within the tight grip Cade had on her and thought she just might go insane if they didn't let her come soon.

She had never hung on the edge of a climax before, the suspense was making her gasp and moan, and there was a distinct possibility she was going to start crying soon. Both men recognized that she'd reached her limit at the same time and acted on it. Cade released his bite to suck her tongue deep into his mouth and swirl it with his. Then Trevor swooped down to do some tongue swirling of his own. His fingers went back to the twisting curving flex on her g-spot and she came with a scream after only one swipe.

That was when she discovered there was a difference between a g-spot orgasm and a clitoral one. The g-spot orgasm was completely overwhelming and devastating, and brought forth a flood of moisture from her body that she actually felt splash onto his hand. Her hips jerked again, but Trevor was ready for it and pulled back to keep his teeth from hurting her a second time. He gave a growl to let her know her disobedience hadn't gone unnoticed.

Trevor pushed away from her with barely contained ferocity and began yanking his clothes off. Cade slid out from behind her on the other side of the bed, and Riley lay there naked and quivering in the aftermath.

Her gaze locked on Trevor as his body was revealed to her. Her brain was clouded and didn't allow her full thoughts, but words like roped and chiseled came to mind. His chest was adorned with a soft looking mat of sandy hair, unlike Cade's crisp black, and rippled with glistening muscles. When his jeans hit the floor Riley gulped. His shaft wasn't quite as long as Cade's but it was thicker and rounder. So thick she wondered if she could fit her hand around it. Without thinking, without remembering she wasn't supposed to move without permission, she reached out to try to see if she could. Her cool fingers wrapped around him just under the head and sure enough, her thumb and middle finger only touched when she squeezed. It flexed and swelled in her grip, and she squeezed harder to see if she could get any other fingers to touch. His whole body tensed, and he thrust once into her grip before his fist closed around her wrist and pulled her away from his body.

"That's it, little one," he all but growled at her. He tugged until she turned over and was flat on her stomach, her arm stretched above her head. He reached behind the headboard with his free hand and pulled out a black rope of some kind that was attached to the post and had what looked like a hair scrunchie on the end. He had her wrist secured before she had a chance to comprehend what was happening. Then Cade got her attention because he grabbed hold of her other wrist and put on an identical strap that was attached to the other post.

She felt a real shiver of fear slide down the middle of her back and tested her restraints. She had some give. She could pull herself up to her elbows, but just barely and not all the way. She looked from one naked gorgeous man to the next wondering what she was supposed to do. Although it went against logic and she should probably be in fear for her life, she wasn't. It was fear she felt, but it was a fear like being at the top of a rollercoaster or watching a scary movie. There was something coming, she just didn't know what it was.

Tonight everything that they'd done to her had been delicious and mind blowing. What was she going to do? Or more importantly, what were *they* going to do to her?

Cade and Trevor watched as Riley's head whipped back and forth between the two of them. Cade smiled when she finally gave up and rested her forehead on the mattress and closed her eyes. It was a sign, whether she knew it or not, that she saw them as equals and therefore didn't know who to look to for direction. She could not have pleased him more. He'd had no idea how important it had been to him that she accept both Trevor and himself until this moment, and something tight in his chest loosened. He looked up from her to Trevor and when their gazes met, he saw that Trevor recognized the significance of her posture and was just as pleased with it. Too many of the women that they'd shared had been the girlfriend of one of them and only accepted the other, it was a rare woman indeed who considered herself equally theirs.

Trevor motioned with his chin for Cade to continue. Cade sent him a dark smile and bent to put the blindfold he was holding over Riley's head, when she jumped and tried to avoid it he murmured, "Sshh. Be still." He gave a gentle kiss to her forehead and smoothed her hair before standing back up. "You're safe, I promise. But you got hurt because you wouldn't obey, and we won't put up with that. Every time you don't do what you're told, you will be punished. Every time."

Riley took a deep breath and tried to force her muscles to relax. She didn't completely succeed but hoped she'd get brownie points for trying. She would have given anything to know what was happening or what was going to happen, but didn't have the guts to ask. She heard a cabinet open and close and then one of them threw something to the other and it was caught with small snapping sound.

"Oh God," she squeaked and heard two identical male chuckles.

Trevor flexed the leather-covered paddle in his hands while Cade twirled his like a pro with a tennis racket. Both men then focused on the lush curves of her ass and moved into position.

Smack!

Riley screamed as her left butt cheek was engulfed in flames. Her whole body jumped with it.

Smack!

She screamed again when the right one went up. Smack, smack, smack, smack.

One after another, stinging and burning, but underneath it all something in her was responding to it. It hurt like crazy, so much so that her head kept shaking back and forth, but with each slap she also felt a clench in the walls of her oversensitive sheath, and she could feel her thighs getting wet from the juices flowing out of her.

Then it stopped. Riley lay there with her ass throbbing so hard she was sure it must look like a cartoon thumb that had just been hit with a hammer. Her breath panted in and out of her lungs like a bellows, and then she heard them. They were both breathing just as hard as she was and she could swear that she could actually feel the weight of their hunger. She moaned and flexed until her ass arched up in the air. There was a powerful rush that swept from her head to her toes when both men groaned at her action.

Trevor was so turned on he was afraid he was going to blow before he even got started. The way she had screamed during the spanking was identical to the way she had when she came. It was hot, throaty and had a purr to it that made his stomach clench with need. She smelled so fucking good and her scent had gotten stronger with each swat, communicating this was a girl who liked getting her ass paddled.

He could tell it was a new experience for her—there was nothing practiced or artificial about the way she moved or sounded. She had opened herself to it, to them, and let herself embrace what they could bring her. It was like an aphrodisiac to him, making him feel drunk, powerful and privileged. He grabbed a condom from the bedside cabinet and thought about the talk that they were going to have about health conditions and contraception, hoping like hell this was the only one he would ever have to wear with her.

He kneed his way between her thighs and felt another surge of pleasure when they parted without resistance for him. Cade briefly snagged his attention when he climbed to the head of the bed and positioned himself against the headboard with Riley's face between his thighs. Trevor looked down at the lovely, juicy peach of her ass, curled his fingers into claws and lightly raked his fingernails over the glowing pink cheeks.

Shivers raced up her spine and though she moaned, she managed to keep still. "Good girl." He praised her for remembering not to move. While Cade took her face between his hands and brought her mouth to his shaft, Trevor gripped her hips and shoved into her to the hilt so that they filled her at the same time.

"Ah shit! She's fucking tight. Oh God, sugar, you feel so good." Trevor pulled out then slammed back home with a grunt of pleasure and warned, "Man, Cade, I'm not going to last. It's been too long, and she's too fucking much." He managed to peel his gaze away from the sight of his cock sliding in and out of her to meet Cade's look over the back of the woman they shared.

"Don't wait for me." Cade's voice shook along with his whole body as he fucked her mouth. He had one hand holding her head still by the hair while the other braced against the mattress and his hips flexed up and down in an increasing rhythm.

Riley was beyond the ability to think. She was lost to the joy and rush of having her body completely taken over. The shaft slamming in and out of her mouth was full and hard, and it was hot the way he throbbed and pulsed against her lips and tongue. The one filling her to bursting between her legs was also throbbing and the way Trevor kept changing his angle and scraping the head against a different spot with each thrust was quickly making it impossible to hold still. Her muffled cries were getting wilder and louder and just when she thought she was going to earn herself another spanking for moving, her body shot into overload and froze. Every muscle in her body locked while it felt like a bomb went off inside her.

"Holy fuck," Trevor yelled as she clamped, then spasmed around his dick, pulsing stronger than he'd ever felt from anyone. The sensation was the last he could stand, his back arched and his whole body flexed as his own orgasm was pulled from deep inside him in pulsating waves of heat.

When it hit Riley, her teeth had scraped and then clamped down close to the base of Cade's shaft. He'd already been fighting to hold back and wait for them, and the pleasure and pain of her bite had him shouting at the ceiling while he filled her mouth with his come.

"Whoa." Trevor shook his head to try to clear it. "What the fuck was that?" he asked as he pulled out of Riley and flopped backwards on the bed. Cade was slumped over sideways himself, "That. Was. Riley." Cade smiled drunkenly at her blindfolded face resting on his thigh. "Told you you'd love her." His hand smoothed her hair and then gently slipped the blindfold away from her eyes. She was limp as a rag doll and with the exception of her heavy breathing she hadn't moved a muscle.

Riley took in the scene at a glance. The three of them lay like puppets whose strings had been cut...and speaking of strings, "Can someone untie me?" She had a drunken smile of her own as the two men were jolted out of their slouches and rushed to untie her with murmurs of "poor baby" and "we're sorry, sugar" while they kissed and massaged her sore arms.

Cade left to get a washcloth for her while Trevor grabbed the covers and tucked her in before sliding in next to her after he'd thrown his condom away. Cade came back and started gently wiping the sweat and other fluids from her face and chin. She smiled at his tender handling of her. Trevor slid a hand under the covers and was stroking her body from hip to breast to belly and back again in a soothing calming motion while she lay on him because he'd pulled her so close. Cade dropped the damp cloth on the floor and climbed in on her other side to sandwich her between them. He tangled his legs with theirs, and his still semi-hard shaft was snuggled into the curve of her waist. Trevor's was nestled under her opposite hip and then with just a few twists and adjustments they all sighed in comfort.

Cade picked up her hand in one of his and toyed with her fingers.

"Unlike me," he began, "Trev's a do-gooder and spends his time in third world countries trying to get malaria." Cade felt her smile and softly chuckle against his chest.

"Unlike you?" Trevor interrupted. "Don't listen to him, little one. He will do his best to convince you he's some kind of jaded satyr when the truth is he gives just as much to charity as I do. And, by the way, he's the one who got malaria, not me." He smirked at his friend while Riley watched the exchange between them wide-eyed and fascinated. Trevor smiled at her and went on. "It was in Uganda and he was there building a clinic." Riley looked properly impressed and gazed at Cade with a mischievous twinkle in her eye.

"Don't look at me like that," Cade told her with a shake of his head as he brought her hand up to his mouth to kiss each fingertip. "I was only there because he was and there was nothing to do that summer anyway. We were out of high school and unlike some of those in our acquaintance, we didn't care to spend another summer sightseeing."

"Like I said," Trevor cut in again, "don't buy into that crap. He's one of the good guys." Trevor's smile faded to a serious contemplation of her face, and he added, "But I guess you knew that or you wouldn't have trusted him enough to let him bring you up here." Trevor's hand settled under one of her breasts and gently cupped the full mound in his palm so he could trace lazy circles around the crest of it with his thumb.

Riley nuzzled her cheek where it lay on Trevor's shoulder and gazed at him with trusting honest eyes when she answered, "Yeah, I guess I did. I guess I trusted you both." Then she yawned with enough gusto to show him her molars, and Trevor decided that as well as loving her body he could easily grow to love the rest of her along with it. "Let's get some sleep. I feel like I could sleep for a year, and you look like you need to." He gave a soft pinch to her nipple and smiled when she arched into the caress even as her eyes started to droop.

Chapter Four

Riley had always been a morning person. She never used an alarm clock because she was awake before it went off anyway. She woke alert and bright-eyed and ready to take on the day. When she woke up a mere two hours after they had gone to sleep, she'd gamely closed her eyes and tried to will herself back into oblivion.

It didn't work. The lazy lassitude was draining away from her limbs, and her natural energy was quickly taking its place. She thought the best thing to do would be to slip out quietly so they could get some more sleep. But how? Trevor was spread-eagle, face down on the bed with one arm draped over her waist. Riley's cheek was pillowed on his shoulder, and she had one leg draped across his butt. Cade was curled along her back with one of his legs tucked under hers over Trevor's thighs and one of his hands was scooping her breast. Just how, she thought, was she supposed to move without waking them? Before she could even try Cade's voice graveled out from somewhere above her. "Go back to sleep. It's early." He shifted his leg higher under hers and gave a gentle squeeze on her boob. Trevor grunted.

Riley tried for all of about two seconds before she admitted, "I can't."

"Yes. You can." Cade again, another squeeze, this one

firmer. Trevor grunted louder.

"But I can't. Honest." Her voice was a soft whisper of apology. "I can never sleep in. It makes me nuts. Besides, I have to pee," she added with a small squirm. "I'll slip out so you guys can sleep, and I'll have breakfast waiting when you get up, okay?" Cade gave up with a groan and a stretch that shook the whole bed. Trevor lay as if he were paralyzed.

"Fine. We'll get up. Trev? Get up and run Riley a bath, I'll start the coffee and order some breakfast."

"Oh no," Riley said, truly sorry that they felt they had to get up with her. "I can occupy myself for a couple hours. Please don't get up for me." It did no good. Cade gave her a big full-body squeeze then rolled out of bed and walked naked from the room. He called back on his way down the hall, "Trevor, get your lazy ass up and go run her bath." Regardless of the harsh words, Riley felt the warmth in them and smiled as she scooted off Trevor's back.

Trevor let out a groan and pulled his pillow over his head. "A morning person?" he grumbled from under the pillow. "Here I thought you were perfect."

Riley lifted a corner of the pillow to peek in at him. "You look cute with your face all smooshed," she teased. "You don't have to get up. I can run my own bath." One eye opened to look at her and she saw it was a lovely bright hazel, nice when matched with that wavy brown hair of his. In a move so quick she yelped, he went from paralyzed sprawl to bouncing up to a crouch over her. "You think I'm cute, huh?" Then he kissed her, morning breath and all. Surprisingly it wasn't unpleasant. "All the girls do," he bragged and charmed her right down to her toes when he rubbed noses with her. "Stay. I'll call you when the water's ready." He walked out of the room naked. Riley sighed deep and long and sent up a little prayer of thanks.

While Riley soaked in a tub big enough to be called a pool, Cade and Trevor talked over their first cup of coffee.

"At first, I thought I was going to kill Gary for letting in an innocent like her. I went out to make a round and there she was. Sitting at a privacy booth—of all the places she could have picked. I swear it was like she had a spotlight shining down on her head." Cade paused as he remembered how angry he'd been at Gary, and how concerned he'd been for an innocent in danger.

"Shit," Trevor said. "I don't even want to think what would have happened if you hadn't gotten to her first." "Yeah, exactly," Cade replied. "So I ream out Gary and then head over to get her the hell out before she could get hurt. You know when I got to her Senator Baxter was there with one of his brat-boys?"

Cade shuddered. Baxter's taste mostly ran to young boys and drag queens, but when he got an itch for a woman his preferences were brutal rape games that only the really hard-core girls would play.

"Christ," Trevor said, and Cade saw him blanch.

"Anyway. All it took was one look from her and I was done. Game over." Cade's smile turned self-deprecating and he sheepishly admitted to Trevor, "I showed her what the privacy booth was for." That said more about Riley's impact on him than any words could have.

Trevor pushed his coffee to the side and leaned toward his friend. "I hope that means what I think it does."

Cade said, "It does." The two of them started making plans.

When Riley walked out a half hour later her muscles were deliciously loose thanks to the hot water and the salts Trevor had added to her bath. She'd found a black silk robe hanging from the doorknob and slipped it on, thankful that they hadn't wanted her to come out to breakfast naked. It was miles too big and the slinky material shifted and slid around her whenever she moved. Her hair was wet because she hadn't been able to find a hair dryer, but she had put on a little bit of make-up and spritzed on some of her perfume from her purse so she didn't smell like Epsom salts.

She found them at the huge dining table. It was loaded down with enough plates to feed a dozen people. They had each put on jeans but nothing else and looked like rumpled beefcake models. Riley swallowed audibly and hoped they couldn't tell she was drooling.

They turned to look at her, and their intense stares and laser-like focus started other parts of her anatomy drooling. Cade held out his hand to her, and Trevor held out the chair between them.

"I was about to come get you," Cade said as she sat. "The food just got here."

"How do you like your coffee, little one?" Trevor asked pouring her a cup while Cade picked up a fork and loaded it with a bite of a scrumptious looking omelet.

"Oh me? Well, as my mom says, I like a little coffee with my cream and sugar."

Cade made a face at her and Trevor smiled in triumph. "See? I'm not the only one." Cade shook his head at them. "How can you even taste the coffee with that crap in it? Here, open up." He fed her the omelet and Riley hummed in pleasure.

By the time she swallowed, Trevor had a bite of ham in front of her. She took it and said around a mouthful, "I can feed myself, guys."

"Shush," Trevor said and took a bite himself. "Let us baby

you. It's what we like. There will be times when we let you feed yourself. But you must always wait for us to tell you to, or else." The or else did not need to be elaborated, and Riley shivered and squirmed in her seat. He gave her a sip of coffee and then Cade brought a bit of apple-filled crepe to her lips and started talking. Both men put one hand on each of her knees and pulled them gently apart.

"For starters, always sit with your legs open. We want to be able to touch you at any time. And, we're keeping you. Ssshh, listen. Just listen and eat. You can ask questions later. After breakfast we'll go and get your things. What you don't need we'll put in storage. After that Trev and I will take you shopping, we're looking forward to dressing you. From now on, we'll be picking your clothes for you. You will wear whatever we lay out for you without question."

While Riley sputtered and tried not to choke, Trevor cut in. "You don't go anywhere without one or both of us. We run our own businesses and have pretty flexible hours but there will be times when we both have to work. Those times we'll either tuck you in with a couple of good movies or take you to work with us." Both men fed her and themselves with one hand while they each kept the other hand on her thighs. Rubbing higher and closer to the part of her that was getting wetter by the second.

"Wait. Wait!" Riley exclaimed, throwing up both hands to hold off the food. "This isn't fair. I can't think. You guys can't say these things to me while you're feeding me and touching me. I can't...ahh." Her hips shot up as each man chose that moment to thrust their middle finger deep into her. Riley's head fell to the back of her chair and her hands scrabbled for a grip on their shoulders as they worked their fingers in tandem in and out of her. One of them, she couldn't tell who, added smooth circling swipes over her clit and her ass arched clear off the chair. Cade and Trevor ordered at the same time, "Hold still."

"I can't," Riley panted. "I can't."

"You can," Cade said against her cheek, "and you will. Or we stop." Then both hands froze on her. "Oh. Oh. Please," Riley begged, her body throbbing around the fingers lodged deep inside her. "Please."

Trevor groaned in her ear, luxuriating in the feel of her contractions on their fingers. "We'll give it to you, little one. Just promise you'll hold still. We can't have you hurting yourself again."

"Okay, okay, I'll try. Just please, please don't stop." Riley willed herself not to move and all but purred as they resumed, increasing the tempo they were playing between her legs. Her nails dug deep into their shoulders in an effort to keep still.

"God, Ry!" Cade exclaimed as he leaned down to run his tongue over one of her exposed nipples. "So beautiful. So fucking beautiful. Come for us, baby. Come, and let us catch you." Trevor chose that moment to latch his mouth on her other breast, and Riley screamed in an orgasm that went on forever.

Both men gently moved their hands to her thighs and resumed eating. Riley lay sprawled in her chair like a drunk and waited for the world to stop spinning. When it did, she dragged herself upright and closed her robe, the look on her face daring either one of them to comment about it. They each raised an eyebrow at her while they chewed, but since she kept her legs open they let her have her little act of defiance. "Now," she began, "you can't just keep me. I'm not some stray cat that you've picked up off the street and have decided is yours."

Trevor squeezed her thigh. "You purr like one." Cade chuckled and agreed. Riley blushed but went on. "Look. This kind of stuff isn't real. It just doesn't happen."

"I beg to differ," Cade interrupted and offered her a sip of orange juice.

"Not to me it doesn't. I have a job. A good job with benefits and a future. Not to mention the little fact that I just met you both less than a day ago." Her voice turned sad and they stopped eating to focus on what she was saying. "What happens to me when you guys decide enough is enough? What happens if you find a new girl?"

When they both opened their mouths to protest she held up her hands to stop them. "I know that you've done this before. There's no guarantee here that you won't do it again. Then what? You both will be fine. Nothing about your lives will have changed. But me? Me, I'll be without a job or an apartment and nowhere to go." She actually felt tears well up in her eyes and didn't state that she'd also be heartbroken. They didn't need to know that part. They wouldn't believe that her heart was already involved, or worse they would and would use that information as a tool to get their way.

"Stop."

Cade couldn't take it anymore. He had wanted to let her have her say, but she was getting herself tied in knots and he didn't like it. "We know what we're asking you to do. We know you are the one taking all the risks. I could wish it were different but that doesn't change the way things are. You trusted us this far. You can keep trusting us."

Cade motioned for Trevor to continue. He was angry and that wouldn't help get them what they wanted. He was used to taking what he wanted, not coaxing or bargaining for it. Trevor was the more diplomatic of the two. He would let him explain it.

"Listen. We will keep your apartment for you. We will pay your rent a year in advance if you're worried about it. It will always be there for you to fall back on. As for work, we thought about that. You can either quit, or take a leave of absence until you realize this is for keeps and then you can quit."

Riley stared at him like he'd spoken in a foreign language. "Those are my two options? Quit or wait and then quit? Are you serious?"

Cade set his cup down with a snap, and his hand on her thigh tightened with a commanding grip. "Yes. Those are your options. We don't want you working. We are not going to limit our access to you around banker's hours. Besides, we both travel, quite a lot and that means you will too. You can hardly expect us to go out of the country without you, can you?" Cade reined in his temper, and spoke as calmly as he could. "Of course there are no guarantees. All you have is our word. Our word that we both want this. That we both want you." His hand cupped her face, and Trevor rested his chin on her shoulder. "We aren't doing this lightly. In fact you are the first we've ever wanted to stay with us on a permanent basis."

"It's true," Trevor added. "The other girls have always had their own place. They'd stay for the weekend or maybe for a cruise or some trip. But they always had their own place. Even Lexi, a girl we dated for over a year, never stayed with us longer than one month. That was for a tour of Europe for her birthday. You're different, Ry. Don't know how. Don't know why. We only know that you're ours."

When Riley shook her head no and was about to object again, Cade kissed her. A full heady kiss meant to prove the words Trevor had spoken and then said, "Say we're wrong and you're right. Let's assume we don't know our own minds and this all fades in a month and we want you out. It won't happen, but if it does, what have you lost? Nothing. Your precious job will be there and your apartment. So you see, you have no reason to resist us like this."

56

Riley looked into his electric-blue eyes and saw the sincerity there. They were serious. They really wanted to keep her like a puppy or a shoe. This was like the *Twilight Zone*. But oh, what if she did stay? They were making it sound so normal and possible.

"Well, how about a compromise?" She looked from one to the other and saw identical frowns of suspicion. It looked like these boys weren't used to hearing words like compromise. "I have two weeks of vacation before I have to start work. I would love to stay here for that time. With you both. But after that, we'll see. Okay?"

Trevor slapped her thigh and said, "All right. Good." Cade however glowered at her and said, "Fine. For now. Let's go shower before we shop."

"Oh. Great. But you two go ahead. I bathed in the tub. I'll clean up the dishes while I wait." Both men looked at her like she was crazy.

Trevor stood and spoke first. "We know you bathed. The bath was for you." Cade scooped her up by the waist and headed for the bathroom while he said, "The shower is for us."

Chapter Five

Riley was standing in front of a bank of mirrors in the largest dressing room she'd ever seen. They were in the fifth store of the day and had already bought her enough clothes to dress an army.

Earlier, the guys had taken one look at her dinky apartment building and had a fit. It had no security, was in a rough neighborhood and it was so old and run down they were sure it would be condemned before the year was out. They'd ranted on and on while she'd packed up what she thought she would need for two weeks. She didn't know what the big deal was. It was what she could afford and even though it was not a high-rise penthouse, she thought it was cute. They insisted that they were finding her a decent apartment to keep for her safety net, because no matter what happened, they were never going to let her come back to that shack. She smiled at the warmth that flooded her at the thought.

Cade and Trevor were seated not far from her, assessing the millionth dress they'd picked out for her to try on. It was black, tight and so short she was afraid her butt cheeks were going to peek out with each step she took. It had a low, deep, vee neck that dipped practically to her belly button. It fit like a glove and she had to admit that she looked like sin on a stick, but the problem was she didn't think she'd ever have the nerve it would take to wear it in public. When she said as much they'd both ignored her.

The same way they had ignored everything she had said about the clothes she was trying on. She sighed and tried to wiggle the hem a little lower, then smiled slyly when she heard them hum in appreciation on the way she shimmied. They told the waiting sales clerk they were taking this one too, and she was off to try the next one.

She took her time changing into the next outfit as images of the morning flashed in her mind. As the men had pulled off jeans and adjusted the six-headed shower—boy, was that a creation worthy of the gods—they had asked if she was on the pill. When she'd said yes, they had practically cheered. Along with everything else, regardless of how smart it was, they'd taken her at her word about her health as she had taken them at theirs. Then they'd pulled her into the shower with them.

She looked at herself naked in the mirror of the changing room and ran a hand over her breasts. She lightly touched on the marks they'd left on them, causing her nipples to tighten. Then she touched on some of the other marks they'd left on her tender flesh. Her hand drifted down between her thighs, and she watched as she slid her fingers between the wet lips. Cade and Trevor had each filled their hands with liquid soap, and she'd stood still for them while they rubbed and tugged and washed every inch of her body. Then Trevor had pulled her back and filled his hands with her breasts. Caressing, squeezing and pulling on them while he'd kissed her endlessly.

Cade had knelt in front of her and placed her foot on one of his knees. He'd smoothed a thick layer of foam over her pubic hair and had shaved every millimeter of that area. She had never known shaving could be so erotic. By the time Trevor had urged her to her knees in front of his swollen shaft she'd been begging for them to take her. He'd tasted different than Cade, felt different in her mouth. He was so thick she was afraid she was going to scrape him with her teeth. Trevor had never taken his hands off her face, running his fingers over her cheeks as they puffed in and out with her motions. It had been so sexy the way he'd kept tracing his finger around her lips as she sucked on him. Cade had been on his knees behind her, and he'd slid inside with a groan. It had felt so different, so much better without that layer of latex between them. She remembered with a shudder the way it had made her come so hard and so fast. When she did, she'd screamed her orgasm around Trevor's thick length and started sucking him franticly, and as deep as she could get him in her ecstasy. Before long Trevor had shouted then pumped, and pumped into her as he came too. Cade's grip became almost brutal on her ass, and he'd started shoving hard into her, causing spasms that lasted forever while he'd followed them in his release.

"Riley." It was Cade's voice calling to her.

She came back to the present with a little gasp of shock. She was naked and leaning against the mirror with her hips working against her own fingers. All while her boyfriends and a sales clerk were right outside the door waiting on her. Oh, shit. What was happening to her? She never masturbated. It had always left her feeling embarrassed whenever she did and usually hornier than before she'd done it. Now, here she was doing it in public? After some of the best sex she'd ever had. God. Maybe they were making her a nympho.

"Umm. Coming," she called out shakily to them.

She heard Cade murmur, "We know." And Riley knew that they knew what she had been doing in here and stood frozen in panic. How was she supposed to go back out there and face them? Maybe if she just stayed in here they would just go away and let her die of embarrassment.

Cade told the sales clerk they had all they needed for now and sent her to box everything. Then he looked at Trevor. They had sat through this for hours, being tortured by seeing her in one sexy get up after another. Legs and luscious ass showcased one minute and then that mouth-watering rack of hers displayed the next. She'd twirled, posed, and flirted with them without a bit of shyness. It had been like a red flag dancing in front of a couple of bulls. Then she'd gone into that damn changing room and hadn't come back out. Within a few short moments, they heard the rustling and slightly wet sounds that could only mean one thing. Her soft sighs confirmed what didn't need confirmation. At first, the image that came to Cade's mind of what she was doing and how she must look doing it was so hot he'd been shocked into silence. Then he recognized the sounds that indicated she was about to come, and he had managed to croak out her name in warning.

Trevor had to clear his throat and brace his hands on his knees. He opened his mouth to speak, but only a groan came out. He couldn't remember being this turned on in his life. The little vixen was going to pay for it. They were in a public place. Not that the public part concerned either Cade or him very much. It was the security cameras everywhere that prevented them from being able to deal with it here and now. Oh yeah, she was going to pay for this big time.

"Get out here, little one," he managed to get out after a couple of deep breaths to clear his head. "Now."

"Um, okay," Riley said meekly. Both men ground their teeth. She peeked out at them before opening the door all the way and coming out. She was back in her red party dress, the ruined straps tucked out of sight. It made the front keep slipping and show her bra, but since the men seemed to like that she tried not to let it bother her. As she got closer to them, she noticed that they were not shocked and repulsed as she had feared they would be. Instead, they looked aroused, and angry. Not mean angry, but intense angry. Uh-oh.

Riley flushed with the awareness that she was going to pay for this, and pay for it with a vengeance. Quick as lightning, each man grabbed onto a wrist and bent her forward until her eyes were on a level with theirs.

Cade spoke, his voice the deep gravel she had learned meant he was highly turned on. "I thought you understood. That is ours. You need to come; you come to us to do it for you."

Trevor tugged to get her to look at him. "You are going to get punished for this. For turning us on like this in a place where we can't do anything about it."

Riley didn't say anything because there was nothing she could think to say. But her whole body was humming like a tuning fork and, if they thought their words were scaring her, they were in for disappointment.

They each kept a grip on her wrist as they walked through the store to pay for Riley's clothes. Cade dropped her hand long enough to complete the transaction and order everything delivered to his place. Then he grabbed her again, and they marched her out the doors.

Trevor looked to Cade and said, "The townhouse is closest."

Cade shook his head and answered, "The little tease likes public displays of affection. I say we give her one." Riley stopped dead in her tracks and almost stumbled to her knees because they just kept walking. "Wait. No. I do not. Not like that."

She started tugging in earnest because they didn't seem to be paying her any mind. "Hey! That's not fair. I don't know what came over me. Sheesh. I haven't known what's come over me since I met you two. It's just that I was looking at all the love bites and then I started thinking about the shower and well...well it just kind of took over... I swear I didn't even realize I was touching myself until you said my name, Cade."

Both men stopped, and Cade swept her up in a furious kiss while Trevor grabbed a handful of her ass and kneaded. Cade broke the kiss and spoke nose to nose with her. "We know that. Why do you think we're so turned on?" They started walking again.

"But but...then I'm not getting punished right?"

Trevor shot her a look full of fire. "Of course you are. You need to learn to control yourself and wait for us."

Then they turned and took her into a restaurant.

Chapter Six

It was a dark, classy place with a candle on every table and the rich spicy smells of Italian food filled the air. A maître d' hurried over and spoke in rapid Italian to them, a big simpering grin on his face. Riley thought she would fall over when Cade answered back in the same language.

They were led to a table in a back corner booth. She was surprised when the two men sat side by side after they seated her on the outside curve of the booth. Her mouth fell open again when Trevor ordered for them in Italian just as fluent as Cade's had been.

"Don't look so surprised, Riley," Cade said to her. "Remember we went to the same schools."

"Oh, yeah. That makes sense." Riley looked around and didn't quite know how to ask what she was thinking. After fidgeting for three endless minutes while they stared at her from across the table, she broke. "Would you guys tell me why I'm way over here? Is this part of the punishment? Not being able to touch you?" It certainly felt like a punishment to her. It was shocking to realize how quickly she had gotten used to having their hands on her constantly.

Instead of answering her, Trevor asked a question of his own. "Are your legs open, Riley?" The way she snapped straight up in her seat was answer enough, and Trevor *tsked tsked.*

"Just batting a thousand today, aren't you?" The silence continued until the food came. There were only two plates and the waitress didn't know what to do with them until Cade spoke to her, in Italian, and she smiled put the plates in front of the boys and left.

"What did you say to her?" Riley asked.

"That you'd be leaving soon so you decided not to eat," Cade answered as he scooped up a huge bite of pasta and cheese.

"Riley," Trevor said without looking at her. "I believe I dropped my napkin under the table. Will you get it for me?" Then he dabbed at the corner of his mouth with his napkin.

As she just sat there staring at him in shock, Trevor took another bite of pasta and added, "Cade's too." Riley looked around the restaurant. She was afraid everyone would know what she was doing. It was dark. They were in the back corner booth. The table was tall with a thick red tablecloth that pooled on the floor and now she understood why the boys sat side by side. They weren't so close that it would look suspicious, but close enough.

There was smooth mood music pumping out from somewhere—Tony Bennett if she wasn't mistaken. The music was loud enough that it made sense to sit close so you wouldn't have to talk too loud to be heard. Oh God. Everything was foreign and decadent—it just kept getting more and more amazing. Could she do this? She had just learned how to do what she was pretty sure they wanted her to do, but she liked it.

She loved the way it felt to have that smooth hard flesh in her mouth. It was amazing how it throbbed and pulsed and burned between her lips. She loved the smell and taste of her two men, each earthy and musky but also with their own distinct essence. Most of all, she loved how powerful she felt that she could bring them shuddering and shouting the way they brought her. Yeah, she could do this.

Before she lost her nerve, she yanked up the tablecloth and dropped under the table.

She scooted to them and reached a hand to each of their knees. She pulled and brought their legs together until she had them sitting spread-eagle. For a second her courage left her and she rested her forehead on their knees in despair. Who was she fooling? She couldn't do this.

She shook her head where it rested and felt Cade's touch on her cheek. His fingers were a gentle caress, tender and soothing. It was not a demand to get on with it or even a caress of desire. It was affectionate, loving, and the simple brush of his fingers told her that if she couldn't do this, it was okay.

Trevor smoothed his hand over the back of her hair, conveying the same message, and Riley's courage and desire came back with a flood of emotion that got her moving. She reached up and tugged open the flies of both men's pants. They had dressed in slacks today, both loose fitting, and she was grateful as she was able to get their shafts out without any problems. Her hands slid up each cylinder of flesh in smooth firm strokes, and her breathing became heavier as they grew under her touch. She tightened her fingers around them and started to pull in faster glides over the hardened flesh. Both men shifted and tilted their hips forward for her.

She smiled in satisfaction when she heard one of them not quite stifle a moan. Then she leaned forward and took Cade deep and fast into her mouth all the way to the back of her throat. There was no tickling swipes of her tongue, or starting at his head, she swallowed him whole and almost came herself when his whole body jolted and she heard him swear. One.

Two. Three deep, hard suckling times down his shaft with a little tongue swirl at the head. She pulled off and slammed her mouth down on Trevor. He jolted as much as Cade and she heard his muttered, "Holy shit, little one," as she sucked him just as hard and deep as she could get him. Back and forth between the two she worked, so turned on she felt little rivers of her own juices trickling down her thighs as she worked them over.

She never took her hands off them. When she had her mouth on one, the other was getting firm tight pulls of her fist. She paid attention to them as she went and noticed that Cade liked it when she added an almost pinching twist to the head between her thumb and her palm when she was stroking him, and Trevor shivered every time she let her fingernails scrape a bit at his base.

Four strong swallows on Cade, then three on Trevor. Then Trevor got five and Cade got two, trying hard not to set any predictable pattern, knowing that keeping each guessing when her mouth was coming back and how long it was going to stay had to be adding to their excitement. With a deep tongue swirling pull, she lifted off Trevor and back onto Cade. She gave him three hard glides to the back of her throat. She fisted her hand tight against her lips and tried a twisting slide of her wrist as she went up and down on him. She was just about to pull off and try that out on Trevor when Cade's leg muscles bunched like steel, and she felt his shaft swell just before he shot off and it splashed against the back of her throat. She heard his groan and a thump against the table but was too far gone with her passion to care if he was attracting attention.

As soon as the flow ebbed, she pulled off him with a soft pop and tried out her wrist twirl on Trevor. His dishes clattered with the first twisting stroke down, and his hand came under the table and gripped her hair. She was trying to keep her hand gentle on Cade now that he was done, but it was hard when she was still so hot and still working to bring Trevor too. It didn't take long. He liked her new trick. Four suckling, twisting pumps and he filled her mouth with his come while his whole body trembled for her.

She slowly eased back and continued to soothe and pet at their softening flesh and tried to will her body to relax and stop throbbing. Trevor and Cade reached down and closed their flies. They reached for her next and brought her up to sit between them.

Cade felt like he'd just been turned inside out. They had thought to teach the little minx a lesson. That she would be there for a moment, then they would pull her up so they could go home and finish what she'd started in the dressing room. At first she'd lost her nerve and they had been about to help her up, but she had found the courage somewhere and set to blowing their minds along with their cocks. She'd learned quickly, and he shuddered as his mind flashed on that last stunt she'd pulled that had him going off like he was fifteen again and had no control. He felt a little dizzy and gave up trying to act cool to lean his head back against the booth until the room stopped spinning.

Cade lifted his head from the back of the booth and leveled an intense stare at Riley's flushed face. She was panting, and her lips were swollen and dewy. She had her gaze locked somewhere in the distance and hectic color bloomed on her face. She was obviously embarrassed and probably wondering what they thought of her. She was such a joy to him. So new to this kind of passion yet so open to it. Embracing them and their desires. She had trusted him from the first second and that kind of naivety was both heartwarming and frightening to him. She trusted them not to hurt her and to protect her. It was a trust he wouldn't see broken.

"Riley." When she wouldn't look at him he repeated, "Riley." Her gaze shyly lifted to meet his and with his eyes never leaving hers, he kissed her with all the tenderness he possessed. He sat back and brought a club soda with lime up to her lips for a sip. He watched her throat swallow, and his eyes squinted as he flashed back to what they'd shared, what she'd been swallowing, and lust again stirred in his blood.

Trevor adjusted her legs and Cade smiled when he heard him say, "Damn, little one. You're wet half way to your knees." When Riley moaned and squirmed to bring Trevor's hand where she needed it most, Cade said, "No, sweetheart. This is part of the punishment. To make you burn for us the way you made us burn for you." He ran a finger from her lips down to the shadow between her breasts. "There's nothing you can do about it."

Riley groaned and felt like crying. She was so hot and turned on and everything in her wanted to scream with the pressure that was built up inside of her. But no matter how she wiggled or pleaded, they wouldn't kiss her again. They took turns feeding her from their plates until they were satisfied that she had eaten enough, paid the bill and led her out the door.

The walk to Trevor's townhouse really wasn't that far, but it seemed like it took a year to get there. It was evening and dark, but from what she could see it was a glorious old building. It was furnished in wood tones ranging from a light tan to a deep black walnut. There were some soft buttery yellow and shades of blue to add color, and Riley thought it looked like a page right out of a decorating digest or something. They didn't give her time to look it over, but instead pulled her upstairs and into the master bedroom. Or to be more exact the master closet. It was the biggest closet she had ever seen. It had floor to ceiling racks and shelves and enough clothes in it to open a store. If her guess was right, this closet was bigger than her bedroom at her new apartment. Moreover, it had a floor to ceiling mirror on the back wall. She stood in the middle of the closet and turned to look at them as it started occurring to her just what they were doing in here. Without speaking to her, the men tuned on their heels and left, only to return moments later each holding a chair.

"Now, sweetheart," Cade said as he sat and crossed one ankle over the other knee, "why don't you show us just what you were doing in that dressing room."

"What? What?" Riley looked from them to the mirror and felt her cheeks flame. They sat side by side, Cade with his legs crossed and Trevor spread out in the classic man sprawl. Waiting. Waiting for her to masturbate for them. Did this never end? Would she forever be shocked and tantalized by every word out of their mouths? Her body was still on fire the way it had been for hours. Not having a release since this morning's shower, she was intrigued and excited by the idea of showing them what she'd been doing. She wanted to watch them while they watched her. Wanted it so much she felt a new rush of moisture between her legs. But... "I have never done anything like this..."

"Like what, sweetheart?" Cade asked, seeming absorbed in a search for hangnails on his fingers.

"Never put on a show or whatever this is..."

"Just show us what you did. Talk us through it. Step. By. Step." Cade's gaze lifted from his contemplation of his fingers to blast her with the heated look on his face. Riley's breath took on a rapid shallow pace and her nipples tightened.

"Well, at first I just went in and took off my clothes," Riley began.

"Oooh," Trevor said, "I love a story that begins with you taking off your clothes." Riley made a face at him and stuck out her tongue. Then she slowly reached behind her to slide her zipper down and let her dress pool at her feet. The strapless bra was gone next and she was naked since they had refused to let her wear any panties. Both men stared at her exposed body with hungry avid gazes. Devouring her with their gazes from her pink-tipped toes to the fiery blush staining her cheeks. Riley worked hard to keep her hands at her sides and tried to act like she was naked in front of fully dressed men every day.

"Go on, Riley," Cade urged in a soft compelling voice. "What happened next?" Riley made a sharp half turn to look in the mirror behind her, so she was standing in profile to them and the mirror.

"I don't know what came over me. Honest. I saw this." She lifted her hand to the dark hickey where her neck met her shoulder. Then her hand slid slowly, gently over her chest and down the slope of one breast to the perfect set of faint teeth marks that spanned the bottom curve of it. "And this," she continued, losing her shyness and caution as her hand brushed on every new mark that adorned her body. "And this one. And I thought, oh this one is Cade's and this one is Trevor's. And this one? Who did this one? Or whose fingers made those prints here on my butt?"

She tilted a little and curved so that cheek of her ass was displayed to them. Her hand went to a bright purple mark high on the inside of her left thigh, almost where her thigh met her pussy and she widened her stance to show the mark clearly in the mirror. "What about this? Which one of them bit me here?"

She looked at them in the mirror, her hand running in light circles over the sex-bruised flesh. It was making gooseflesh appear all over her body and sending chills racing from her fingers out. The men were transfixed, and she stopped thinking

71

this was a show. This felt as intimate to her as any encounter they had shared so far. They were as elemental a part of this as her hand. Her fingers tipped with pink polished nails drifted over her newly shaven mound. "The skin here is sensitive, and it felt good to run my hand over it, like this—" her fingers trailed light circles over the outer lips, tickling, "—and it looked nice too. I've never looked at myself here. I thought, I don't know, I guess I thought it was pretty." Another blush came to her cheeks as she admitted this in a whisper.

The men responded with affirming murmurs. "I liked the way it felt. I mean the skin was soft and damp, and I liked the way it felt to touch myself, and then I kept remembering this morning and what you both did to me, and I slipped my finger inside...like this" There were three groans as her tiny middle finger slipped thru her labia and disappeared into her wet channel.

Riley's breath got choppier as she continued. "Ahhh, and...umm...I, uh, then I did this..." Her finger slipped back out, wet and shiny and circled her clit. Her knees gave a little, and she leaned against the mirror resting her whole side against it while she moved her finger in faster circles and dipped in and out. The men said nothing as she worked her hips against her hand while those fingers slipped and slid over her wet glistening flesh.

Her movements got sharper. She was breathing harsher as her climax got closer, and Riley started to moan, lost in the erotic thrill of watching them watch her while she did this forbidden thing. Her head fell back with a groan as she dipped two fingers inside and with two sharp thrusts, she came, flushing and panting while her body ebbed and flowed against the mirror.

Her eyes had closed with her climax, and she didn't hear the men come over. She felt Cade first as his mouth covered her fingers and his tongue slid between them to press against her clit. Trevor was behind her, his hands spread her ass cheeks and his tongue ran in a wet hot line from the base of her crack to the base of her spine. His grip was strong and amazing as he massaged and squeezed her cheeks while his tongue and lips and teeth covered every inch of her backside. Cade dipped two thick fingers deep into her slit, pulled them out and plunged his tongue in and then switched again.

Almost as if they'd planned it, Riley was turned, and it was Trevor who had his tongue on her clit and Cade who bit and sucked on her ass. They turned her again and Trevor slipped one long hard finger up her tiny back hole. Riley screamed in a mind-blowing blast of ecstasy that had her coming in a flood over them, her knees giving out, but the men wouldn't let her crumble. They kept her upright, and Trevor added a second finger to her small tight hole while Cade started to suck hard and fast on her clit. It was amazing. The orgasm kept pulsing, throbbing and blasting through her as her muscles clenched around the fingers that were buried deep inside her. Before long, it was too much, and Riley thought she was going to go insane from the overload.

Cade stood, keeping his fingers buried deep and whispered fiercely in her ear. "We're going to fuck you back there, Riley." Riley's knees buckled, and she would have fallen if not for the men's grip on her. "We're going to fuck that tight little ass of yours, and you're going to love it."

Cade pulled out of her pussy and hooked his hand under one of her knees. He brought that leg up high, and Trevor crawled under her and started to suck on her throbbing clit. The fingers of his one hand were lodged deep in her ass, and he used two fingers from his other to pump an opposite rhythm in her pussy. Riley's head whipped back and forth on Cade's shoulder as he bent to her breasts. He tongued the hard tips and sucked them as though his life depended on it.

"I can't!" Riley panted. "No more. Oooh!" Her nerves were too raw, and she thought her mind might break if she had another orgasm. Cade growled and bit into her breast. Hard. Trevor spoke against her quivering flesh, "Just one more, baby. Just give us one more from this sweet pussy." Then he added a third finger to her clenching dripping sheath and scissored the two fingers he had in her ass. That was it. Every muscle in her body seized, and she shot up to the tips of her toes in an orgasm that screamed through her system like a hurricane.

In the aftermath, the men soothed and caressed her, making shushing sounds as she continued to pant and jerk with aftershocks.

After the men undressed, Cade picked her up and carried her out of the room while Trevor jogged ahead and opened doors for them. Two turns down a hall and up a flight of stairs and they were in a glass atrium bursting with plants. In the middle of the room was a huge hot tub. Riley thought she'd died and gone to heaven when Cade stepped in with her and sat in the steaming water with her on his lap.

Trevor was on the other side of the room, and she was just about to ask what he was doing when hundreds of soft twinkle lights gleamed on. The hot tub jets started up, and he was coming back to them. She smiled while she reached a hand out to him. At first he tried to sit on the other side of the tub, but Riley was having none of that and tugged until he was close enough that his thigh touched Cade's. She leaned forward to kiss him, long and deep while she held Cade's arms tight around her middle. She wiggled and shifted until she was practically floating over them both. Her head bumped against Cade's shoulder while her butt floated and bobbed against

Trevor's lap.

She fell asleep that way and would have drowned if not for Cade's hand holding her head up. Trevor traced lazy patterns around her bobbing breasts as he spoke, keeping his voice low so he wouldn't wake Riley. "We're going to kill ourselves at this rate." He sent Cade a look that let the other man know he would die happy. "Have you ever seen anything like her in that mirror? My God, we're two lucky sons o' bitches." His voice was almost reverent.

"I've never seen anything like her with everything she's done." Cade's voice was just as reverent as he met his friend's gaze. "How many girls have we shared? Twenty? They were good right? Great. So why, I ask you, is it that I can't remember a damn one of them? Why does it feel like every time we touch her and everything we're doing is the first time we've done it?"

He shook his head wondering why a man, who didn't believe in love at first sight, was suffering from it. He was a practical man. He had been head over heels because of a girl so many times he'd lost count. He'd always loved women. They both had. He reveled in the newness of each one that came along, the adventure of discovering the secrets that each woman's body held. However, it was the same sense of discovery he felt for, say, a new artist he'd stumbled upon, or a new culture that fascinated him. It was exciting and fun, not earth-shattering. Not life-changing. But this, this was unlike anything he'd ever known. He never bought into this crap. He ran a club that thrived on debauchery and on any given night over half of its occupants were married and there without their spouses.

He came from a healthy family with two parents who were devoted to each other, and Trevor had the same thing so he knew that there was such a thing as happily ever after. But he also knew that was rare. It was a life he had never seen for himself. Until now and he'd only known her for a day. He also knew Trevor was suffering the same transformation that he was. "I feel like I'm in some sappy movie and any minute Julie Andrews is going to start singing." Cade smiled at Trevor, and the two of them sighed in contentment and held onto the one woman who had changed their entire world in just a small handful of hours. "It's ironic, don't you think?" Cade asked. "This morning we thought she was the one whose life was being turned upside down. That she was the one who was taking all the risks."

Trevor grunted in agreement and said, "To think we almost missed her because we were going to take Annie out." Cade nodded at that. They shared one woman at a time—they did not take on multiple partners. If they had started dating Annie, he would not have been free to act on what Riley brought out in him, no matter how much he'd have wanted to. He just sighed deep again and thanked God he hadn't asked Annie out last night like he'd planned.

Chapter Seven

Ann Tucker was pissed. Her thoughts were an angry roiling boil as she stewed in the employee lounge and silently ranted. *I hate working here in this stupid restaurant,* she thought to herself. *I hate having to simper and smile at all these hypocrites.* For over a year now she'd worked at a job she hated. "For what?" she muttered out loud to the empty room, "For a shot at being the one to be served for a change. Dammit, I know it was finally supposed to pay off tonight. Tonight I know, *know* that it was supposed to be coming to an end."

Tonight she was sure Cade was finally going to ask her out. Then the bastard hadn't come in. It was well past the dinner hour and therefore well past the end of her shift, and he was a no show. She'd planned this for too long and worked far too hard to sit back and take this.

She had known Cade and Trevor since she was six years old. Her father was groundskeeper at the Marshall's summer home. She had grown up in a dinky two-bedroom apartment above the Marshall's five-car garage. The place was only one of the Marshall's many homes, she thought bitterly, and yet they were so stinking rich they could afford to keep her father there year round to make sure the house was pretty and perfect for them whenever the frickin' urge came over them to breeze in for a stay. Jeez it really burned her that they could come and go from one home to the next whenever they fucking wanted to. It wasn't fair she thought, why should they have so much when she had so little?

She stormed around the room in her tantrum and stopped in front of the full-length mirror on the door to look critically at her reflection. She was tall for a woman, five ten, and she had the lanky, slinky build of a runway model. She liked how svelte she was and often went without eating to ensure that she stayed willowy. She ran her hand along her side and felt pride in the fact that she could feel each rib. Every woman on earth wanted to be skinny like her, but nobody she knew was quite this slim. She tugged on her skirt and tried to get a good look at her ass. It was small and even if it was kind of on the flat side, she shuddered at the alternative. The latest craze of big butts just did not make sense to her, and she was sure it would pass. Nevertheless, until then, she had taken to wearing shaper pantyhose that added lift and padding to her rear.

Satisfied, she turned her attention to what she considered her best asset, her breasts. They were small, tight and perfect. She opened another button and pulled until the shirt gaped open and her breastbone gleamed out from between them. They were a small perfect A cup. So small that they stayed right where they were without a bra. She was a looker and she knew it with her white-blonde hair and green eyes. She didn't care that the blonde came from a bottle, brightening up the otherwise mousy brown. She also didn't care that her natural eye color was a much softer and cloudier green than what the contacts gave her. It didn't matter, everyone wore contacts and colored their hair. It didn't change the fact that she was hot. Her lips were a slim pink line, and her father had paid a fortune to make her teeth white and straight. There was nothing wrong with her. So why wasn't Cade asking her out?

She had done everything she could to make this happen.

She had begged and pleaded and pouted for months until her father gave in and asked Cade's dad to get Cade to give her this job. At first her dad had balked, telling her that she needed to earn things on her own and that he was sure she would get the job if she just applied herself...and yadda-yadda-blah-blah. It took forever, but he'd finally given in and she started. No interview, no hassle and no chance that he would turn her away.

As she went back out front to pretend that she even cared about the others and getting the last of the dinner crowd out, she continued to stew behind her super sweet smile.

She had wasted a whole year pretending to be the proper well-placed young lady she thought he would like. Her clothes were professional, and she acted as sweet as candy to anyone and everyone whenever he was around. Wanting him to make the moves, that way he would feel responsible and feel he had to take care of her. But after the longest, most boring year of her life, she'd snapped and couldn't take it anymore. She had tightened and shortened her skirts until she could hardly move in them, and she'd stopped wearing her bra. Her little breasts poked at her blouses and bounced softly whenever she walked. Cade had noticed from the very first night. He had stopped dead in the middle of his phone call and swept his gaze from her head to her toes, stopping appreciatively at all the right places. He hadn't said anything to her that night, but after that, he came in every night she worked and that was new.

Last Tuesday Trevor came in with him and they sat at a table. She knew about them. Of course, she knew. She had made a habit out of spying on them the whole time she'd been growing up. They were almost six years older than she was, so she was never on their radar. They always saw her as just some harmless little kid, most times they'd just smiled at her, and never minded if she hung around. Sometimes she would slip into the boathouse and hide in the rafters and listen as they talked, practically drooling with envy as they talked about the places they went and people they knew.

Then, one week before she'd started hounding her dad about getting her a job here, she'd heard them talk about a woman they'd shared.

They had talked about how hot she was and how good she was in bed. Cade had said how he wanted to get her something, like some painting she'd liked. Trevor said they should get her a collar, since she liked being led around by one so much. In the end Cade had said he was going to send her that painting and Trevor was getting her the collar, a diamond one. At first, Ann had thought the woman was just some slut, but the more they talked, the more she had come to see that they didn't think she was. They'd talked about her as if they liked her. They thought she was wonderful, and Ann decided right then that no matter what, she would be the next woman they thought was wonderful. She would be the one they were buying presents for. Moreover, she would make sure they kept her for a lot longer than they had that other woman. She would make damn sure her claim on them was lifelong.

So when Cade had brought Trevor in she knew what he was up to. He had wanted Trevor to check her out. To see little Annie grown up. At first, she had simply led them to the table and seated them. Prim and proper, pretending she didn't know her skirt was so tight it was about to bust at the seams, or her boobs were all but falling out of her opened-down-to-there shirt. But when they just continued to stare at her as she walked back and forth she'd thought, fine I'll make this move too, stalked up to the table they were sitting at, slapped both hands down on it and leaned forward. Her shirt gaped open, and she watched as both sets of eyes had riveted to her exposed breasts. She'd smiled, liking the way arousal had tightened their faces, and had spoken in a throaty voice she'd hoped went straight to their crotches. "What's the matter, gentlemen? You haven't ordered yet. Isn't there anything here you want?" Trevor had laughed a little, but Cade had just lifted his eyes and stared at her, hungry. "Not tonight. Perhaps this weekend."

She knew that this was supposed to be the night. Only, her shift had been over for an hour, and he had not come in. What the hell? She could not chase after them. She would not make any more moves. They had to do it. If she made the moves, then they would think that she had asked for it. Then they wouldn't feel as responsible for her as she wanted them to. As it was, she had already made it clear that she was open to them both, which was already off from her plans.

She had planned to act shocked and reluctant to their twisted demands. She had planned to make them beg and woo her into it. She had planned to make them take turns for a couple weeks first and beg and plead to her before she let them do it to her together. Then she was going to cry and act fragile. They would be thankful to her for letting them do that to her, grateful. She wanted them to be mad for her. She wanted them to be absolutely insane for her, giving her more presents than they had ever given any other girl.

When she was tired of them, when she had gotten enough from them, then they would give her money that would last forever...or at least eighteen years.

A kid that they would both pay out the nose to see had the same luxuries and benefits that they had. It was a drastic step she knew, but the kid would be with nannies and boarding schools just as they had been, so it wouldn't bother her too much. It would be worth it. Because the mother of their child would rate the same lifestyle as that child. As close as they were, and considering that they both would be sleeping with her, they would both take responsibility for her and the brat—

that meant double the money.

It wasn't as if she hadn't been knocked up before. Of course, those times had been taken care of in a nice uptown clinic. The desperate daddies had paid nicely to make her and the problem disappear.

But this was no small-time banker or stockbroker like she'd usually gone for, these were two of the country's most precious trust-fund princes. She was not going to have them slip through her fingers after all she'd done to get this far.

"Hey, Mike?" She snagged one of the bus boys cleaning up a table, ignoring the way he jumped when she picked him out. "Have you seen Cade lately? Or heard why he hasn't come around this weekend?"

Mike ignored her and kept cleaning up the table.

"Hello?" Ann snarled with a shake of her head. "I asked you a question." Jeez. What was with this guy any way? No wonder she didn't talk to the other workers, they were just a bunch of rude nobodies. She stomped off to find someone else to ask. That little prick probably didn't know anyway. He was just a busboy for crying out loud, what would he know?

She reigned in her temper and sauntered up to Gary when he came in from the club. She knew that Cade and he were friends so she always made it a point to be nice to him. She flirted with him a little and did things like bring him his favorite drink whenever he came in for his breaks. She smirked at him when his eyes bugged out at her outfit, thinking it was funny how easy it was to make a man want her.

"Hey, Gary," she said as she got close to him. "Want me to get you a drink?" She brushed a delicate hand across his forehead and smoothed his hair back. "You look like you could use a break. Is it crazy over there tonight?" Gary smiled and started talking about what was happening over there, not even guessing that she couldn't care less. She caught herself at the last minute from rolling her eyes and just nodded and waited for him to stop talking so she could ask him what she wanted to know. "Gary," she interrupted when she couldn't stand hearing him drone on one more second, "um, I'm sorry, sweetie, but have you seen Cade around? I mean, he's usually in here every weekend when he's in town, and I haven't seen him since Tuesday."

Gary leaned in close to her and smiled. "He was in last night. You didn't see him?" She perked up and shook her head no. "Well, he must have hit the club before the restaurant. I don't blame him for not coming in. You wouldn't either if you had seen the little number he hooked up with last night."

"What?" Ann shouted, not caring if heads turned her way. "What the hell are you talking about? What number?"

"What's up, Ann?" Gary leaned away from her. "What's it to you?"

Ann quickly schooled her features to look curious instead of pissed and tried to soothe his ruffled feathers. "I'm sorry. I'm sorry. It's just such a shock. You know we grew up together, I uh, I'm just a little protective of him is all. You know, his mom would skin me alive if I let her little boy get hurt." Ann almost gagged on that whopper. His mom hadn't paid any attention to her since she was ten. But Gary didn't know that, none of these people did. She had always led them all to believe that she was practically one of the family. It helped keep them in line and off her back about work.

"Oh. Well, he can take care of himself, and he never struck me as a momma's boy," he said.

"He's not," Ann insisted and leaned in to squeeze his arm and brushed her braless breast against it. "God, can you imagine Cade as a momma's boy?" She laughed silkily and shifted so that her shirt slid open just enough so one puckered pink nipple peeked out at him. "Never. But his mom would love it if he were. When she found out Cade wanted me to come up here and work with him, she took me to the side and hinted that it would be nice to know that her baby had someone she trusted looking out for him."

It was a plausible story and she knew Gary would buy it, not having any reason to doubt her.

"Now, tell me about this little number so when his mom asks me about her I can say I knew all about it and put her mind at ease."

"Man, she was hot. You don't have to worry about him. She looked as fresh and innocent as Christmas snow. If you should be worried about anyone, it should be her. She looked like an angel out there and Cade—" Gary bent to whisper to her so no one would over hear, "—took her into a privacy booth and—"

"No he didn't," Ann interrupted, feeling the bottom fall out from under her. "He never uses the club. Even if he finds someone, he takes them up to his place."

"Oh, he took her all right. I was kind of keeping an eye out on her 'cause I wanted to make sure she didn't get hurt. So I was watching her, and Cade just walked up, ordered them drinks and activated the privacy shield. Afterwards, he marched her to the elevator and told the manager not to bother him for the rest of the night. Nobody has seen him since."

Chapter Eight

"Kincade here." Cade's voice was gravely from sleep. It was only eight in the morning according to the bedside clock, and he could think of nothing short of death that would make this phone call acceptable. After soaking in the hot tub, he and Trevor had brought Riley down, dried her off and then tucked them all in for the night. It had only been about eleven at that time, but after the lack of sleep the night before they were as beat as she was. He wouldn't even have answered his cell if it weren't the restaurant's number.

"Hi, Cade, it's Annie."

"Yeah, Annie, what's up?"

"Hey, boss," she said, her voice dripping with apology. "I feel so bad about calling you, but I didn't hear from you or see you this weekend. I just wanted to make sure everything was okay. Last night was a little crazy at the club and the new bus boy, Mike? Well, he was making some waves, and anyway, it was nothing I couldn't handle, but I just noticed that you weren't around." She dropped her voice to a purr. "I missed you. I was hoping you were going to come see me last night, I thought that's what you'd said, and well, I just had to make sure that you hadn't fallen under a bus or something."

Cade felt the fog slowly clear from his brain. He had made some overtures to Annie, but he hadn't made any promises. He felt a small twinge of guilt that he might have led her on, but he let that go. Things happen. He had made no promises, hadn't even had a date with her, so she was just going to have to deal.

"No, Annie, no bus," Cade softened his voice. She was just acting on the sparks they had been giving off to one another, and he couldn't blame her for that. "I'm fine. I just got busy this weekend. As for the work stuff, I'll be in this afternoon to check into it." He hung up.

He turned his head and looked at Riley sandwiched between him and Trevor. She was wide-awake. The cell phone hadn't done it, he knew because she hadn't shifted or stretched or even moved when it rang.

"How long have you been awake, Riley?"

"Your heart beats sixty-eight times a minute," she said instead of answering. "You breathe thirteen times in a minute. Trevor is seventy-two and fifteen. Only, every three minutes Trevor's breathing stutters a little, and for that minute he breaths twelve instead."

Cade stared at her, giving her his best boss stare.

"About an hour and a half." When Cade groaned she added, "I told you I was a morning person." Cade ran a weary hand over his eyes, and Trevor spoke against the back of her neck. "My breath stutters?"

She sighed enchantingly, like a contented cat and Cade rolled to his side to face her. Her hair was a chocolate cloud around her head and his arm, the mass so curly and wild it completely hid Trevor's face from him. Her big soft eyes were crinkled at the corners as she smiled at him. She had the cutest nose he had ever seen, it was tiny. He had an insane urge to see if he could fit his finger up it. It didn't look like even a pinky would fit up there.

Before he remembered that he was an adult, a somber, responsible adult, he tried. Yep, wouldn't fit. She squealed and grabbed at his wrist with both hands. "What are you doing?" She laughed. "AHHH! You freak! Get out of my nose! What are you doing?"

She bucked and tried harder to get away as that relentless finger pushed at her nose. "Look at this, Trev," Cade said with a laugh, not remembering the last time he'd played with a girl. "Look. Her nose is so tiny I can't even get my pinky up there."

Trevor loomed up and then his finger was exploring her face. "Let me see. Damn you're right. Guess all your holes are tiny, little one." With another shriek Riley squirmed and tried to lunge herself away from them.

They played and tussled with her until she was breathless—tickling that made her laugh so hard she went silent and wrestling that made her grunt with the effort to break free. She gave as good as she got and found out that Cade was ticklish under his arms and just under his ribs while Trevor wasn't ticklish at all. But he did jump and shout when she yanked on his chest hair out of revenge for his lack of ticklish spots. He'd laughed at her spunk and dove back into the attack with a vengeance.

Inevitably, those tickling fingers started exploring flesh that was ticklish in a different way. A little brushing squeeze on a breast, a featherlight caress across her newly shaven mound that had her arching off the bed. It was a slow build up, roughhousing turning light. Fingers that were digging between her rib muscles to make her squeal slowly shifted to tender brushes to make her moan. Soon she was on her side facing Cade while Trevor was close at her back—all three of them touching from head to toe.

Trevor would arch her head back and kiss her with soul searching intensity while Cade's mouth would explore her neck and shoulder. Then it would be Cade kissing her with his tongue tracing every millimeter of her mouth while Trevor's tongue delved into her ear and his teeth nipped at the lobe. There was tenderness this time. A compelling need to cherish, not consume. The passion had the warmth of a summer meadow instead of the burn of a roaring fire. They loved her with a gentle care that had tears welling in her eyes while desire washed in a lazy wave over her skin.

When they sensed she was ready, Cade and Trevor shifted and both men reached to bend her knee and lift her top leg up out of the way. First Cade's throbbing swollen shaft slipped into her. "Shh. Shh," Cade shushed with his lips against hers. "Oh God, baby. You are so sweet. Mmm, so good. Shh, don't move, let us love you."

Their hands on her thigh was so thrilling, having them hold her and move her, their mouths both working on her neck, mouth, breasts. After only a few gentle thrusts, Cade slid out and Trevor slipped in. His angle stretching her in a completely different way than Cade's and it was glorious to Riley. Her back arched at the contrast between her two lovers. Her mind consumed with the passion and emotion they evoked in her. But they held her tight, not letting her move, not letting her race to climax. Trevor's husky deep voice was hot in her ear as he whispered, "Don't move, Ry. Uh, oh, don't move." His voice broke for a moment to hum in her ear as her inner walls clenched around his shaft. "God, baby, god. I love the way you feel on my cock. Let us take you soft, baby, soft and slow and sweet for as long as we can." Then he shifted out and Cade was back and the angle change again riveted thru her whole body. Riley felt like she was drowning in the beautiful sensations they were causing in her.

Back and forth they went, for what seemed like hours, all the while Riley kissed and caressed them trying to pull them close, wishing she could pull them right into her soul. Gradually, the fires within them grew. The embers sparked to flames, and the melting tenderness gave way to stronger passions that wouldn't be denied.

Cade felt her walls clench in a slow wave that rolled over his shaft like glory. His own muscles clenched as his control snapped and he thrust deep and hard, hitting her womb and reveling in her gasp and moan of pleasure. "Yes," he said thru gritted teeth, "yes, like that." He thrust again, harder. "Tell me you like that. Say it. Tell us you want it."

"Yes." Her eyes were closed. "Yes. I want it. Oh, yes, want you both...oh, both, so much... Ahh..."

Cade's tongue plunged in to her mouth and cut off anything else she might have said as with a groan, he pulled out and Trevor shoved in, jolting her body against Cade's. Trevor pulled her leg higher and angled his body back so he could get deeper inside her. His hips pounding against hers now, as sweat started to run in rivulets down his brow.

"Come with me, little one," he panted thru his clenched jaw. "Let me feel you milk my come from me. Uh," Trevor's voice cracked as he must have hit a spot inside her that was especially good. "Yeah, milk me, Riley, take me with you." He shifted again, and Cade, knowing what Trevor needed as though he were in the other man's head, pulled Riley over until she was practically on top of him.

He groaned as Trevor thrust against them, his over-sensitive shaft was cushioned against Riley's soft belly, and the friction was a sensual torture. He held back, trying to wait until he was inside her again before he let himself come.

Trevor roared, his back arching and his hips pistoning like thunder in reaction to the deep clenching orgasm that overtook Riley. He let his own climax burst from him in all consuming waves.

Trevor pulled out of Riley and pulled her back with him until she was laying on him now. He lifted her knee high, almost to her shoulder and she arched and screamed when Cade drove into her with a growl. Her nails scrabbled over Cade's back in an effort to hang on as Cade pounded into her. He pumped so hard it shook not only her and Trevor, but the whole bed, and banged out a furious tempo on the wall. Her hips were lunging for Cade, trying to meet his ferocious thrusts. She reached a hand back and tangled her fingers in Trevor's hair. Then every muscle in her body locked and she came again. Both men felt it, both men responded to it. Trevor squeezed, hard and added yet another set of teeth marks to her tender shoulder, reveling the way her body responded to them. Cade, caught inside her sheath, felt it like a vise on his throbbing cock. He struggled to breathe while his own orgasm raked like claws in his gut, and he spilled himself in her with guttural shouts of his own.

The three of them panted and twitched like survivors of a lightning strike. Riley took in the whole scene—she had a moment of reverent wonder that these two amazing men had chosen her. Even if for a moment, or a day, whatever time she had with them she vowed to embrace. To cherish these men who made her feel so alive and desirable. She was going to stop questioning herself or their motives and just revel in them while she could, hoping that when it ended she would have no regrets and that her heart would be able to recover.

"I think I'm paralyzed," Riley said. "I can't feel my legs. Is my right one still there, or did you rip it off, Trev?" Riley asked with a poke in his ribs.

Trevor slowly turned his head to look at her, the movement taking all the strength he had. "It would serve you right if you were paralyzed," he said to her. "I think you cracked my spine. God, Riley, you're an Amazon. You're going to kill us at this rate."

With her energy quickly returning, Riley scooted to the edge of the bed and was off before the men caught on to her intent. She crossed her arms under her breasts and smiled at the twin frowns they shot her for leaving them.

"Come back to bed, Riley," Cade said.

"Hey, what do you think you're doing, Ry?" Trevor said at the same time. Riley shook her head at Cade with a smile and answered Trevor. "I think I'm going to cook breakfast. I want you two to stay here and let me do this." She squealed and jumped back when Trevor sat up and grabbed for her. Cade just scowled darker and repeated, "Riley. Come. Back. To. Bed." When she shook her head no and backed up further, Cade started to rise and continued to talk. "You have forgotten your place. It is in bed. Not the kitchen. We have take out for that. You are not going to be fetching and cooking and cleaning for us. That is not why we want you. You don't ever have to lift a finger for us. Now, I won't tell you again. Get. Back. Here." Cade knew he was losing his touch when she didn't show the least bit of fear at his threatening scowl. Instead, she affected a pretty pout for them and twirled a lock of her silky hair in one delicate hand. She made such a pretty picture, her body all rosy and her lip sticking out for them while she swayed back and forth. Even though he knew she was doing it on purpose, he still felt his heart clench with the flood of affection she brought out in him.

"Please? Can I please do this? Please?" She stuck her tongue out at them when she was hit with two pillows. "Fine." Her play pout gone as fast as it had appeared, she placed both hands on her lovely naked hips and glared at them while her voice got serious. "You two can buy me a ton of clothes and feed me and treat me like a princess, but I'm not allowed to do anything for you?" Her teeth ground in frustration when she received two nods in answer to that question.

"C'mon. I love to cook, and I'm a good cook and I hate to disappoint you but I am not good at just lying around like a lump. I have to do something. So please. Let me do this for you guys. I can't buy you guys a mountain of clothes, but this I can do. I want to!" She even stomped one bare foot with that. The effect was ruined though because it caused her breasts to sway and all their attention shifted from her words to her body. Nevertheless, she still must have made her point because when she growled and stormed off to find the kitchen, neither one said a thing to stop her. But she did hear a word of warning as she left the room. "You are treading on thin ice, little one. Careful," that was Trevor. "Ice that's going to crack on that sweet little ass of yours." That was Cade and Riley marveled that the threat of a spanking felt more like a promise to her. A promise that warmed her in places that were still throbbing.

Thirty minutes later Cade and Trevor were seated at the breakfast nook in the kitchen, trying hard to hold onto their resentment of her defiance. It was hard to do when faced with a stack of biscuits that were baked to golden perfection and a bowl that was full of some of the best smelling sauce either one of them had ever encountered. They had agreed to let her wear her dress to cook in, once she'd promised to take it off as soon as she was done. Finally, when the woman who had lovingly prepared the meal was seated between them, naked again and looking eager and excited, it made it impossible to stay upset.

"Before we eat," Cade said while Riley broke open a biscuit and fragrant steam poured out. "I just want to know two things. Where did you get the stuff to make this and what is that sauce made of? It smells like heaven."

Riley flushed with pleasure and ladled a generous heap of gravy over his biscuits. "It's biscuits and sausage gravy. It doesn't take a lot of stuff, thank goodness because there wasn't much there. As it is, I had to make do with canned milk for the gravy 'cause you didn't have fresh. There was sausage in the freezer and the rest of the stuff in the cupboards. Don't tell me you've never had biscuits and gravy?" When she looked from one to the other and received blank stares, she was shocked. "Everyone's had biscuits and gravy. C'mon, you two probably grew up with cooks. Why, this is the all-American breakfast, I can't believe you never had it before." As she talked, she made an equally generous plate for Trevor, and sat back with an expectant smile to watch each man take his first bite.

"Ohmagawd," Cade murmured around his first mouthful. It was a creamy, spicy, gravy with a biscuit that he could swear was melting on his tongue and he didn't think he had ever tasted anything this good.

Trevor didn't make time for words; instead he just grabbed Riley and kissed her full on the lips out of gratitude before diving back in. Riley laughed as she wiped gravy and bits of biscuit from her mouth and watched them eat like they were starving.

"Well," Trevor said after the first couple mouthfuls. "Sure we grew up with cooks. Chefs and gourmets. Whenever we are out with any charity expeditions, it's soup lines and take out. But I don't think either one of us has ever had what you'd call home cooking before."

Cade was already reaching for seconds when he added, "I

can see now that we were deprived children after all." Riley laughed delightedly. As small as this was, she felt such a wealth of pride flush thru her. She had given them something that they'd never had. She sat back, watched and wondered if they were going to remember to feed her or if she should ask.

Chapter Nine

Later that day Riley was still naked. They had showered, and the men dressed and ruled that Riley was not going to be wearing clothes that day. At first, she had balked and felt affronted. She couldn't walk around in broad daylight in the buff. Especially if they were going to be fully dressed. However, her complaints had fallen on deaf ears.

She didn't get used to it, but she did start to see the benefits of it. When she was in the kitchen cleaning up the breakfast mess, Trevor had come in behind her, pinned her against the counter, kissed, sucked, and licked at her backside until she had screamed out her orgasm. Then he had gotten bottled water from the fridge and walked away, without ever saying a word to her.

Afterwards, she'd explored the townhouse and its different rooms. She found the guys in a game room playing pool, and Cade had snagged her by the waist. He laid her out on the green felt table, draped her legs over his shoulders and had licked and lapped at her until she was again screaming. All the while Trevor had watched and sipped from his water, whispering quiet words of direction and encouragement to them. After bringing her to not one but two mind-blowing orgasms, Cade helped her down from the table and shooed her out of the room so they could resume their game. All day she was pressed to walls or dragged to the floor, all for her pleasure. With fingers or mouths they would drive her to one cataclysmic peak after another and then leave her shaken and gasping, wondering when they were going to end the madness and finally take her. Craving the full shattering climax that only came from their shafts buried deep inside her, she knew they wanted to take her. It was evident in their constant erections, and in the way they couldn't keep away from her. But they resisted, and she didn't know why.

About five in the afternoon the three of them were on the couch watching an old movie that Riley loved on TV. Cade and Trevor were seated side by side with Riley stretched out across their laps. Her face was pillowed on a cushion next to Trevor's hip while both men caressed and fondled her bottom and the tender flesh between her legs. It was hard to concentrate because without warning one long finger would slide deep inside her dripping sheath, and then pull back out. Then another would drench itself in the moisture built up inside her and delve deep and fast into her ass. Then it was gone. It was soothing and slow and as she would start to moan and squirm, wanting more, they would pull back. They would rub her back or legs and tell her to be still and watch the movie. It was just another layer to the already catastrophic experiences she had gone thru. Riley worked hard to memorize every moment and sensation that she felt. Hoping that the memories she was building would never fade so that she could cherish this time with them for the rest of her life.

Cade was rubbing small light circles on her clit when Trevor again dipped his finger into her tight back hole. "Damn," Cade said to him, "that looks so good. Can you see that?" Riley flushed with excitement as Trevor shifted to get a better look at his finger dipping into her ass. "Oh, yeah," he replied, his voice deep and sensual, "looks damn good." His other hand grabbed her hip and shifted her so her back arched and gave him a better view. "She likes it. Watch this," he said and Riley felt a second finger stretch her back hole open. She moaned and bit hard into the pillow under her head and tried to keep still. She understood what they were doing now. They wanted her to watch the movie and pretend as if she didn't know what they were doing to her. Every time she responded or moved, they stopped. If she wanted them to continue, she was going to have to be still and act like she couldn't hear them. Or feel them. Or it would stop.

"Oh yeah," Cade said again, his voice dropping to that gravely tone that she loved. "She's almost ready, Trev. It's going to feel so good to take her up that sweet little hole." He smiled and chuckled darkly when her muscles clenched at his words. She was being good though and not moving too much. He slipped two thick fingers into her juicy sheath, making sure to tease at her g-spot. "She's got the sweetest tasting little pussy. Don't you think, Trev? She's wet. Here, listen." He whipped his fingers back and forth fast inside her, slamming against her inner walls and sending ricochets of sensations throughout her body as the wet and juicy sound filled the air. "Mmm, when we take her there the first time," Cade continued, "I wanna do it in the hanging chair. What do you think?"

Trevor twisted the two fingers he had in her ass and groaned as she clenched around them, finding it harder to hold still.

"She's learning to be such a good little sub. Look at her. She's like a drug, and I think we're addicts. Yeah—" another twist and plunge, "—the chair would be perfect." Riley couldn't take it anymore and arched her ass back into those delving fingers with a cry. Slap! Trevor slapped hard on her ass. She arched and screamed, the stinging slap the last straw in breaking her control and the flood of her orgasm poured out of her like a tidal wave.

"Fuck!" Cade ground out. "You weren't supposed to come yet, sweetheart. God, you're a hot little thing."

The ringing of Cade's cell phone stopped him as he was just about to spread her out on the coffee table and slake the lust Trevor and he had been slowly building all day. Torturing themselves with each caress, each taste of her. Holding back their own need for completion, testing each other to see who would crack and take her first. Oh well, he thought, the distraction might be just what he needed to hold back a little longer. Then Trevor would be the one to break first instead.

"Kincade, here," he answered as he admired the way Riley lay sprawled and panting in their laps, keeping one of his hands buried in her quivering flesh.

He listened with half an ear as his manager filled him in on some pretty basic complaints. People calling in sick, the chef they had on was given to fits of temper and had lost it when a customer had requested a dish be made with special instructions, and all the normal things he'd come to expect. With resignation, he faced the fact that he would have to go in. He normally loved the work, the challenges and the excitement of nurturing something that he'd created and developed. Knowing that it was all him. That he had made this success on his own, not by riding on his family's coat tails, was a surprising source of pride for him. However, with the luscious little body currently draped across his lap, dealing with work drama was the last thing he wanted right now.

He looked at Trevor. "I have to go in."

"Wha...? Oh no." Riley turned her head to look at Cade over her shoulder. "Do you really?"

Cade smiled at the look of dismay on her face. She looked truly upset, like he was moving away instead of just headed into work for the night.

"But we, umm..."

"Don't worry, sweetheart." Cade leaned down to lay a soft kiss on one supple ass cheek. "I should be done over there by ten and then we can pick up where we left off." Reluctantly, he slipped out from under Riley and went to get dressed for work. He kept a room and full wardrobe here just as Trevor did at the penthouse. They didn't consider one place belonging to one of them and not the other. Both of them had suites in each place and they came and went depending on which was closest to wherever they happened to be at the time. It had always been the way things were between them.

"We'll keep the home fires burning for you, Cade," Trevor said, adjusting his grip on Riley now that his were the only hands on her.

"I'll bet." He sent Trevor a look that conveyed a wealth of emotion and humor. Then he leaned down nose to nose with Riley. "Don't let him wear you out. I intend to finish what we've started here tonight." Then he kissed her, his tongue filling her mouth the way he longed to fill her body with his. When her hands started to reach for him, pulling to bring him closer, he pulled away with a groan.

Riley flounced down on the couch with a harrumph and looked over her shoulder to Trevor. "Ten o'clock?" She gave him her most beguiling look and whispered throatily, "What are we going to do until then?" She leaned in to slide the tip of her tongue along the curve of his ear and her hot breath shivered down his spine as she went on. "Parcheesi?" She nipped at his lobe. "Backgammon?" Her hand went under his grey T-shirt to scrape her nails lightly across his nipples. "How about chess?" Her teeth bit into the cord of muscle in his neck and shoulder. She shifted until she was sitting on his lap and her bottom was rubbing rhythmically against the swollen bulge under his zipper.

"Little one," Trevor groaned, "you're killing me. Mmm, stop that, ah God." His hands went to her hips to push her away, but instead, when her hot little tongue swept into his mouth, he pulled her closer and helped her straddle him. "You're going to make me lose. Cade is going to crack first. God, baby, God." His hands were clenching like vices on her hips, grinding her hot little cunt onto his shaft hard enough to split the denim between them. His iron will crumbling under her tender onslaught. "Who cares?" she said into his mouth, rubbing her breasts against his chest as she pressed against him. "Besides, how can you call this losing?" Then she added a little rotating wiggle to her grinding and Trevor said, "Good point." Then reached a hand between them to tear open his fly.

His flesh sprang free and he gripped it at the base with one hand while he guided her into place with his other. Both groaned deep when he slid into her. She flexed her thighs tight to his hips and gripped as hard as she could with her inner muscles, working to bring his thick hard cock as deep as she could. Loving that she finally had him in her after hours of incredible tormenting foreplay. Her nails bit into his shoulders and her head fell back, a million nerve endings zinging throughout her body.

Trevor added his strength to her thrusts, plunging her back down onto him every time she lifted up. His stomach muscles flexed like iron, holding back his climax by the teeth as it fought to burst through and devour him. She looked like a pagan goddess above him. Her hair was a curling mass down her back that pooled on his legs. Her breasts, mmm, those lovely perfect breasts, swayed and bounced on her slender frame as she worked herself up and down on him. The tightly budded tips beckoned and he bent forward to catch one in his teeth.

That was the sight that greeted Cade when he came back down stairs on his way out. Trevor still fully dressed, Riley still gloriously naked. One luscious breast caught in Trevor's mouth, her gorgeous ass gripped in his hands as he worked her up and down on his lap. It was a sight that would torture him all night long. Teasing him and bringing a hard on with it every time, he was sure. His only consolation? "I win." He walked over to cup Riley's head in the palm of his hand and leaned forward to steal a kiss from her open, panting mouth.

"Who cares?" was Trevor's reply, echoing Riley's sentiment, never slowing his pace as he looked Cade in the eye. Cade looked down at Riley, his hand tightened in her hair until it fisted and she opened her eyes to fix him with an unfocused stare. "I won, Riley," he sucked briefly on her top lip. "I'm first." Then her bottom lip. He slid one finger around her opening where Trevor was plunging in and out of her. Then that finger dipped deep into her tight back hole, "I get to fuck this first." She clenched on them, his finger, and Trevor's shaft. "Ah, God, Cade," Trevor exclaimed. "Ahh, what are you doing to her?" Cade smiled darkly at his friend, "What's the matter, buddy?" Cade taunted and angled to pump his finger double time into her. "Can't you hold back? Afraid she's gonna bring you too soon?" Cade *tsked tsked* at his friend, trying to ignore how hot it was making him and instead focus on bringing them both to orgasm. "I thought you had better control than this."

"Fuck you," Trevor said through gritted teeth, knowing that he had no chance of holding back if she kept clenching on his dick that way. Her tight inner muscles rippled around him nonstop.

But it was Riley who snapped first. Her hands slapped on

Trevor's chest, nails digging deep, and groaned as her body undulated over him. Cade pushed deeper and flexed his finger in her ass, moaning, he was so turned on. That was all Trevor was waiting for, and his arms banded around her waist while he flooded her womb with his release.

Cade growled and bit into her shoulder as he gently slid his finger from her gripping hole, and then laved the bite with his hot tongue before pulling away. With another growl he stalked to the door. He sent one last smoldering look at the two of them. Trevor had turned Riley until she was cradled like a child in his lap and he was lightly kissing her forehead. Then he looked up to meet Cade's eyes and sent him a mischievous wink. This was going to be a long night.

Chapter Ten

"So little one," Trevor said as soon as the door closed behind Cade. "I'm starved. How do you feel about burgers?" Riley snuggled deeper into his lap and let her eyes drift shut. After the day they had put her through nothing sounded better than a nap right then. Just as Trevor was going to ask her again, his stomach beat him to it and rumbled loud enough to startle her. Riley looked up at him with a smirk and said, "Okay, burgers. But all my clothes were sent to the penthouse. Is there any chance there is something here that we can make do?"

"We'll figure something out." Trevor stood with her in his arms and adjusted until she was clinging to him like a monkey. With her legs wrapped tight around his waist and a death grip on his neck, he started for the bedroom. He couldn't be happier as he headed off with his hands cupped on her bottom. As far as he could remember, nothing had ever felt better than what the three of them had shared these last couple of days. The closeness he shared with Cade was something he treasured and he had always resisted getting too involved with women. He strove to keep it casual, because he'd feared the day when he would have to make a choice between a woman and his best friend. But now, for the first time, he was seeing the possibility of something more with a woman.

Riley welcomed them and opened herself without reservation. She was responsive and eager and even though it was foreign and different, she pushed aside her misgivings and trusted them. She was lively and spunky, but at the same time showed that she loved being dominated as much as they loved dominating her. However, before he let himself get too excited, they were going to see how she fit into the other aspects of their lives. Starting now.

"Welcome to the Lords of Flatbush," Trevor gestured expansively with his arms, a bag of greasy burgers in one hand and the most enormous soda she'd ever seen in his other. They were standing in front of a huge building that looked a lot like a warehouse. It had some thick barred up windows along the front. Across the huge double doors the center's name blazed in florescent writing.

Trevor handed her the bag and opened the door to his pride and joy. He had been raised in privilege. Every luxury, and every convenience, at his fingertips. His parents had always taught him that wealth came with responsibility and duty. Every person was responsible for each other. He'd been raised under their example of charity and community involvement. Family vacations always included an element of work. He had toured the world as a child and seen every beauty that the earth had to offer. And every tragedy. Days spent basking on the beaches of Cabo were followed by days not fifteen miles from those beaches feeding the poverty stricken Mexican children whose lives depended on how many beaded bracelets they could make and sell in a day.

It had touched him drastically to know that while he had laughed, played and eaten until his belly could hold no more, there had been children starving not far away. It was even more shocking when he realized that it was the same everywhere. Every tourist spot, every country, every island, had poverty. His parents worked hard to see that their children saw this and dedicated themselves to doing what they could to live up to the blessings they had been given.

Cade and his family shared the same convictions. Many of those family trips had included both families. It was a long running joke that the two families had come over on the Mayflower together, inseparable from the beginning of time. Charity and community was vital to both Cade and he. If Riley couldn't share in this passion with the same commitment that they had, whatever they were feeling for her would fade. It was an elemental part of who they were. There would be no room for growth between the three of them without that. As his parents always said, 'If a person is shallow, there's no room for roots'.

Riley looked around with awe. The place was a children's paradise. There were arcade games galore, and through an open door, she could make out a rink where two boys were circling each other decked out in boxing gear. She turned huge eyes on him, and a self depreciating smile as she asked, "Can we play? I see the Next Generation pinball over there but I have to be up front and let you know...I'm an addict." Trevor chuckled at her. "Oh yeah? You think I could get you out of here if I let you play?" He leaned down to touch his forehead to hers, unable to resist her teasing.

"Yes. I could stop in any time I want," she sniffed. Deciding not to tell him about the times she had missed out on movies because she could not walk away from the pinball games in the theatre's arcade. "You'll regret it though because I will humiliate you in defeat," she bragged. Then she raced off, darting between games and boys of all ages and laughing like a loon when Trevor called out to the boys to stop her. It was a mad race, and she dodged four of them before one caught her and trapped her against Mrs. Pac man. She was sure she could have gotten away, but was too breathless with laughter to put up much of a fight. Trevor sauntered up with a swagger and swooped down to claim her. He locked one hard arm around her hips and one hard shoulder in her stomach then carried her off like a caveman—much to the joy of the boys watching. There were cheers and catcalls following them as he carried her to the lounge.

As they ate the best burgers that Riley had ever tasted and sipped from the same soda, Trevor told her about the center and how he'd come up with the name. She laughed and told him that it also just happened to be one of her favorite movies. She said it was campy, and he needed to watch it again in order to appreciate the joy that could be had in a truly awful movie. As they talked, Trevor was filled with a fresh wave of hope.

Riley was touched by his commitment and filled with admiration that he had single-handedly brought this together. She was excited that they had this in common, thrilled that there was more than just good looks and amazing sexual skill to these men. She eagerly told him about her own efforts back home, feeling a little embarrassed since her accomplishments would be meager compared to his. But it was common ground for them, something she had been doing as long as she could remember, and she was happy that there would be more than just sex between her and these two.

Trevor tried to keep calm, but a warm kernel of love started in his chest and spread as she continued to talk. She told him about volunteering at food banks with her mother, then about helping in a soup line once a month with her youth group. Her dad was a tree hugger she said, and from him she'd learned a love of nature. Together they had planted trees and did neighborhood cleanup projects every summer. She also told him about the Christmas canned food drive that she had started when she was only a teenager. She'd been a student helper to a fourth grade class and had noticed that more than half the students were poorly dressed and underfed. So she'd gone to the principal and started a food drive. Before long, the entire community had gotten behind it. That Christmas they had raised enough food, clothes and toys that every low-income family in that school had gotten a delivery. It had gotten much bigger than she had dared hope for and a local charity had come to help with the organization aspects, and it had continued every year since.

"That's why I went to work for the bank," she told him. "I needed a good paying job if I was ever going to get out of my folks' house, but I didn't want to do just anything, you know? But volunteer work in Washington doesn't pay, that's why it's called volunteer. Well, I found out about CRA. Do you know what that is?" He did but didn't say anything because he could tell that she was excited to tell him. "It's the community reinvestment act. It means that if a bank is going to be making money in a community, that bank has to give money back to that community. At the bank, I get paid full wages to volunteer. It's the best of both worlds. They don't care what charity I volunteer at as long as I'm volunteering. The bank gets CRA credit for it and pays every employee to do eight hours of volunteer work a week. I get to do the work that I love, and I get paid for it too. Now I can make enough money to live on my own." Then she wrinkled her nose at him. "Of course, I still have to put in time at the bank. But it's a small sacrifice to pay and it's not that bad, I guess. It's definitely worth the trade off."

Trevor could have told her that she was never going to have to work at the bank again, but he didn't. She was so excited he did not have the heart to start pressuring her. They had agreed to give her these two weeks, and he would stick to that. She didn't know it yet, but she had just sealed her fate. She'd shown him the one thing that he needed to see to know that she was in fact the one for them—her heart.

They finished their dinner, and he took her on a tour. The tour didn't get farther than the pinball machine she'd beelined to earlier however. She was as good as she had bragged and proceeded to wipe the floor with him. Before long, they had a crowd and every time she humiliated him, they cheered for her, the traitors. When he gave up, she took on all challengers, and beat them into the dust as well and showed no signs that she was ready to leave. In the end, he'd had to carry her bodily away while she had laughingly protested that she had at least another hour in her.

"C'mon, sweets," he said as he carried her toward the door. "Let's go to the club and see how Cade's doing." Riley panicked at that. The clothes that he had scrounged up for her were an old pair of sweats with a drawstring to keep them on, and about a mile cut off the bottom of the legs. Top that off with the matching sweatshirt that was long enough to be a dress and Cade's club was the last place she wanted to be seen. "I can't go there. Are you crazy? Have you looked at me?" He thought she looked adorable, but he didn't want her in a panic so he told her, "Don't worry. I'll sneak you up to the penthouse. You can change before we hunt him up."

Chapter Eleven

Cade was working hard at concentrating on business. It wasn't easy. Riley's scent clung to him elusively. He would turn his head to answer a question and it would drift by. He would wave a hand to say hello to someone and it would come again. Every time it did, he would see her. He would see them. Her body quivering under his...her mouth on Trevor while he pounded into her from behind. It made him edgy and distracted. He longed to just go back to the townhouse and have one more night with her before reality set in. Surely, work could wait for one more night. Why when they'd found Riley, was it impossible for his managers to handle these problems alone?

Ann caught up with Cade in his office. He was snarling at a stack of invoices on his desk while he reamed someone on the phone. She felt a frisson of desire shiver along her spine at this show of power from him. She walked quietly to his desk, sat her hip on the corner of it and leaned over until she was sure he could clearly see down her blouse. She had dressed with care tonight, picking the colors and fabrics that complimented her most. Her make-up was perfect and her hair was a shiny, chic gloss around her face. She knew she had never looked better, and had enough confidence in herself that she was sure if he would just look at her, he would forget about whomever that little tramp was that he had dug up this weekend. He couldn't be serious about her. She'd let herself get fucked in a booth for pity's sake. For all she knew, he had dumped her already. She reached out one red tipped finger and ran it around the ear that did not have a phone on it. Then leaned forward to whisper in it that she had something to discuss with him, making sure her voice was light and breathy.

"Look," Cade said curtly to the person on the other end of the phone. "I pay you for a specific service. If you can't provide that service to the specific obligations in our contract, I'll find a new company that can." Then he disconnected, cutting off the sputtering of the moron on the other end. The manager had assured him that the shipment of alcohol they had delivered had been verified and signed for. Cade stared at the invoice. It was several cases short, and Annie herself had verified it. He looked at her leaning on his desk. Her long slender body was dressed exceptionally well today and she was again showing him her small pert breasts.

He had never paid much attention to her. She had always just been a shadow around the house. He'd thought she was a harmless little thing, even though she was given to fits as a child. When his father had called him and asked if he had a position for her, he hadn't had to think about it. His father considered hers a dear friend. He had gotten her trained for the work and never had a problem with her. She was professional, if a bit aloof. His managers said she was efficient and on time. He did hear the occasional complaint that she was a bit of a snob, but he'd shrugged that off. Everyone was entitled to his or her quirks.

The relationship between them had been cordial and pure business for the entire year she'd been here. Until a couple weeks ago when she had started dressing and acting like she wanted much more than just business from him. For the first time he had looked at her as a woman. She was a beautiful one, she needed some curves sure, but he was a man who appreciated women in all their lovely forms. He hadn't felt the need to dive right in. He'd instead wanted to feel things out first. Considering the family history, not to mention the fact that he was her boss now, he'd wanted to tread carefully. He had of course wanted to see what Trevor thought. Trevor had been shocked at his first sight of her. She no longer even remotely resembled the dirty little rug rat they remembered. He and Trevor had been reluctant to take her, feeling almost incestuous about it. After all, they had known her since she was in grade school. However, she was beautiful, an adult, and had made it clear that she was open to taking them both. The reality was that she was not related. They had agreed to take her up on what she so generously offered to see where it would lead. Then Riley had appeared and changed everything.

He realized by her posture that she was hoping to start on that offer here and now. He thought it best if he made himself clear and save her from as much embarrassment as he could. He reached out carefully to her gaping blouse and started buttoning while he talked as gently as he could. "I have been meaning to talk to you since I came in tonight. I'm sorry that it's been put off. Things have been crazy this evening." He sent her a sad smile, seeing the way she tensed as he went on. "You are a beautiful woman. I could have swallowed my own tongue the first time I saw you all decked out like this. I want you to know, though, that I have met someone. Someone who is becoming important and that means that I'm going to have to pass on what you are so pleasantly offering." He brushed the back of one hand on her cheek, mistaking the flush that came over it as embarrassment instead of the anger that it was. "I mean what I say when I tell you that I want you to stay. You're an asset to the restaurant. I couldn't be happier with your work here. I know that things might be awkward for a while between us, but I hope that you won't let that ruin the progress you've made here. You should also know both Trevor and I are extremely flattered that you were interested."

Ann just nodded and put her head down. If she spoke, she knew she would shriek like a banshee and ruin every chance she had at getting him to change his mind. She put a hand to her eyes, hoping he would think she was crying, and he would give her some space. It worked. He kissed the top of her head before he left the office, shutting the door quietly behind him.

Instantly, she jolted from the desk. She was so angry she actually stomped in place, repeatedly. She fisted her hands and ruined her hairdo by madly flinging her head from side to side. Who did that sanctimonious prick think he was?

"Oh, we're flattered, he says," she mimicked, like a school yard bully. "Oh, I want you to keep working, blah blah blah. What a fucking asshole." She kept ranting and mocking, so furious she wanted to break his head in. Nobody brushed her off.

Just because he had money didn't mean he could throw her away like garbage, she thought while resentment stewed in her belly. She had to gather herself. She wasn't going to take this. She had watched them date three other women while she had waited for Cade to look her way. Three. Over a year of dragging her ass to work while she'd waited too.

Well, no more.

She was going to do something about this. She had waited long enough, and she was not going to wait until they tired of this one, she was going to get rid of her, and get rid of her now.

Cade walked into the restaurant, guilt nagging at his mind. Maybe he shouldn't have said anything. Maybe if he had just ignored her, she would have gotten the message and backed off. Then he shook his head, it was better this way. Clean, clear and direct. She deserved that from him. He was absorbed in his thoughts and was wondering if he should go back in and see if she wanted to go home for the rest of the night when he stopped dead in his tracks and every thought flooded right out of his head.

Riley was standing by the hostess station waiting to be seated. She was wearing that last black number that they had gotten for her, and her body was beautifully outlined in it. Her luscious breasts managed to fill the deep vee of the neckline without looking like they were about to fall out of it. Her hips were perfectly rounded with the material stretched flat across them, the dress just tight enough to hint at the mound of flesh at the apex of her thighs. Those thighs. Her legs were short but so amazingly formed that he felt his knees go weak just looking at them on display in that short, short skirt. Her dainty feet were strapped into killer black heels that allowed her tiny pink toes to peek out at him.

When he managed to tear his gaze from her body to her face, it was like a punch to his solar plexus. Her lips were painted a deep, mouthwatering red, her eyes a smoky grey and her hair was held back from her temples highlighting the high arch of her cheek bones to fall in curling waves down her back.

She looked like a vision of sensual delights, and he wanted to show her off and hide her away at the same time. It was a confusing mix of emotions, all tangled inside him with a possessiveness that was new to him. He and Trevor normally liked to show off their women, dressing them as scantily as they dared, enjoying the lust that sprang to others eyes when they took them out. Now, he wanted to kill every man who dared to think of her the way that he was, and he caught himself actually glaring at Gary who had come up to talk to her.

Where the hell was Trevor? Cade could not believe he had left her alone in a public place. Just as he got within hearing distance of the two, Gary reached out and ran a finger down Riley's neck. Through the red haze of anger that clouded his head, he heard Gary say, "So I see the boss has staked his claim." Riley pulled back from him with a small smile and was about to say something when Cade snarled from behind her.

"Yes, Gary, I have." His hands clamped onto her shoulders, and Riley jumped and would have stumbled on her ridiculous heels if not for the death grip he had on her. He leveled a stare on Gary that had the shorter man forgetting that they were friends and saw real fear from the other man. "It would be best if you remembered that, and refrain from touching her in the future."

"Cade," Riley's whisper was shocked. There was real threat in his voice. She knew he was a strong man, really that had been made clear this weekend, but the fierce waves of menace that were pumping off him was not something she would have expected. She knew a flirt when she saw one, and she could tell that Gary was a harmless one. His manner was the same tongue in cheek tease that it had been that first night. This aggression from Cade was so out of proportion to what had happened she had the insane thought that next he'd be lifting his leg on her.

She smiled apologetically to Gary and elbowed Cade in the ribs while she did it. Gary did not wait around to see what would happen next, he just left them with a mumbled, "Yes boss," and cleared out of there before Cade decided to follow up with the threat that was plain on his face.

"Well, that was pleasant." Riley turned to face Cade, pulling from his grip. "You know if you didn't want guys flirting with me you should have bought me different clothes. Like jogging suites and muumuus."

Even if Cade was a little shocked at his own behavior he had a point to make. "He shouldn't have touched you. What was he thinking stroking you that way?" Cade's voice had risen on that last, and Riley put her hand on his lips to quiet him. "Jeez, will you be quiet." She smiled at the other couple waiting to be seated.

"He's just a flirt, it was nothing. Besides, look at me. I must have used half a tube of concealer and your hickies still bleed thru. I look like a leper." She said it with a quiet laugh as she leaned in nose to nose with him, the whole situation turning funny to her as she noticed he kept glaring at the men who looked in her direction.

It may be small and completely anti-women's movement of her, but his display of possessiveness was thrilling something deep inside her. Something he would never see. No, sir. It would not do to let him know she liked his Neanderthal antics. She was secretly going to love this side of him though and hoped that Trevor shared this same trait. She had a suspicion that it had to do with the fact that they shared her. If there was any fear that they would be trying to share her with anyone else it was obliterated in the menace that was still pumping off him like heat rays from the sun.

Cade couldn't decide what to say. She was laughing—laughing—and he wanted nothing more than to pound on something. He finally managed to pull his composure together and since they were handy, took Riley's lips in a kiss meant to melt her laughter and remind her of who she was laughing at. It worked. When he pulled back, she was breathless, and her eyes were unfocused. He gave her a brisk nod and said, "We'll talk about this later. For now where the hell is Trevor?"

"Right behind you," Trevor said from over Cade's shoulder. "What's up?" Then he saw Riley, and his mouth literally dropped open. "Holy shit. Little one, look at you." Trevor then pleased her right down to her toes when he too searched the room for any man who might be looking at her.

Cade gave a not too friendly shove to Trevor's shoulder. "What do you mean, look at you?" He glared from Trevor to Riley, not sure who yet, but one of them was going to be in serious trouble for Riley being in here unescorted. "Didn't you see her already? Didn't you bring her in here?"

"No," Trevor said, getting a bad feeling in the pit of his stomach. "I was in the bathroom and Riley said through the door that you two would meet me here." His glare turned to stone on Riley. "You told me Cade was taking you down." Cade clamped one hand onto Riley's wrist while Trevor came around and clamped onto her other one.

"I never said Cade was up there," Riley protested, really getting worried about the anger that they were directing at her. "All I said was, and I quote—Cade and I will meet you in the restaurant. Then I came down here to find Cade. It's not like I had to travel across town to find him."

Cade bit out thru gritted teeth, anger boiling his blood, "I made myself clear to you the first night what kind of club I run here. The restaurant is fine, but you had to walk through the club and around the building to get here. Do you realize what could have happened to you? What kind of danger you were in?"

"Well, what have we here?" Ann's soft voice floated into the tension filled air. There was a cat-like smile on her face as she took in the scene. She couldn't be happier to see them so ticked at the little slut. When she had first spotted her, Ann had felt the bottom drop out of her stomach. There was no denying that she was a pretty little thing. But she was short, and to Ann she looked as fat as a pigeon. She was one of those women that Ann could never understand why men liked. Big boobs and a butt that stuck out to there.

Ann was angry that the men she had set out for had betrayed her for this short, round thing, then she had noticed their anger. They were pissed at her about something, and Ann made her way over as fast as she could in hopes of finding out why.

Cade quickly schooled his features and relaxed his grip on Riley. In public was not where they were going to deal with this. They needed to get her home and soon. This was too important to delay. Cade had images of horrific scenarios flashing thru his mind about what could have happened to her on her way thru the club. Without a doubt he knew Trevor was having them too.

"Annie," Cade said, as formal and calm as he could get under the circumstances, "I'd like you to meet Riley. Riley say hello to Annie. She's a long standing friend of Trevor and I."

"Hello," Riley said, not sure exactly what she was feeling. One part of her was scared, not just about what the guys were going to do, but about the things that Cade had said too. She missed completely the measuring look on Ann's face because she was so preoccupied with her own thoughts. "Nice to meet you, Annie—"

"Please," Ann cut in, "call me Ann. Only family calls me Annie." She gave Riley a knowing smile that penetrated her distraction, "And very close friends, of course."

"Oh, of course." Riley forgot all about the pending doom headed her way and focused on the slender blonde in front of her. The woman was smirking at her as if she thought Riley was worse than pond scum. She didn't know where the anger was coming from. Did this woman scorn her because of what she was doing with these two, or was it because she wanted to be doing it with them instead?

Before she could ponder it too long, Trevor got her attention. "I thought we could maybe do a little dancing and have a night cap while we waited for you. But Riley is tired. I think we'll head up and wait for you in the penthouse."

"Good idea," Cade said and bent to whisper in Riley's ear. "Prepare yourself, sweetheart, this is going to hurt." Then he walked away with his hand cupped lightly on Ann's elbow. Perversely, Riley was more upset about the way he was touching the other woman than his threat.

"C'mon, Riley," Trevor's voice clipped in her ear. "You might not enjoy where this evening is now headed, but I know we will." Riley couldn't help but notice that Trevor's hand was clamped on her elbow in a much harder grip than Ann had received from Cade and felt a little spurt of jealously.

Chapter Twelve

As soon as they stepped off the elevator Trevor gripped a fistful of her hair and pulled until she was on her toes. Riley felt a sizzle from the base of her scull to the base of her spine. She had never thought herself the kind of girl to enjoy pain, but the way they wielded it was a fine mix of sensations that brought a gasp to her lips and a rush to her privates. "I can't tell you what kind of danger that you put yourself in, young lady. You are going to learn to obey. When we tell you that you are not to go out in public alone, we mean it." He released her with a suddenness that had her stumbling forward on her pencil thin heels. She would have fallen if not for Trevor's reflexes as he reached out and steadied her. As soon as she was standing on her own, however, he let go again and spoke to her in a voice that was pure disciplinarian.

"Remove your clothes and get on your knees." He stood back with his arms crossed over his chest and a scowl on his face as he watched her reach shaking hands to the shoulder of her gown and slip it down. He could not meet her eyes. He was so angry he thought if he looked her in the eye and did not see understanding about the danger she had placed herself in he would snap and start yelling. It was much better to focus on the flesh she was slowly baring to him. As soon as she had removed the dress, she was naked. The garment had a built in bra, and Trevor had not laid out panties for her tonight when he'd picked out her clothes. When she went to remove her shoes, Trevor's grumbled, "leave them," stopped her. She slowly lowered herself to her knees and looked up at Trevor.

"Little one, what's you safe word?"

"Spinach."

"That's right. Remember that. If things get too much for you, that's the only thing that will stop us."

Riley's expression turned to confusion and bewilderment. "But Cade said that if I said it, it would end everything and I don't want to leave." The tears that filled her eyes did more to calm Trevor's anger and also tugged at his heart. "No, Ry. That word will only stop whatever action we're doing. It won't end us. Not after the first night. If a girl needs to use the safe word the first night, her desires aren't a good fit for ours and it's best if it ends there. But you didn't use it the first night did you, little one?" He smiled like a villain and said, "In fact you've never come close to needing it because you were made for us and every time we come together just proves it more and more."

Riley smiled at him as the confusion melted away from her expression, and her eyes sparkled at him with eagerness.

"We're turning it up tonight, Riley. You have got to learn we won't take chances with your safety. Now, wait right there until I tell you to move."

Trevor felt his anger shift to desire as she waited for his next order. She waited with big liquid eyes and a quiver on her tasty lips. Her nipples tightened as he watched, making his mouth water. She was waiting to do his bidding. Trusting him in whatever he decided to do. He felt a completely new level of desire while she knelt there, quietly as he let the time stretch. He had enjoyed being a Dom for years. That balance of trust and exchange of power was exhilarating in a way that few people understood. But from Riley, a woman who had no experience in this realm of sexual expression, it was intoxicating. She had the ultimate power, the power to stop everything and deny him. It made each step he took a tight wire act. The need for control was warring with the need to lose that control. Trevor walked away from her, knowing that she would not move until he told her to. He went into the master room to prepare.

When Cade stepped off the elevator twenty minutes later he knew where to find them, and he showed no outward reaction to the sight that greeted him when he stepped into his bedroom. Riley had her hands bound in leather-padded cuffs, and her arms were stretched above her head, a velvet rope attached from them to the swivel in the ceiling.

She was tied into a black satin corset. Trevor had cinched it tight, until her waist was impossibly small. It thrust her breasts out and curved lovingly over her hips. She was blindfolded and standing submissively in the same amazing strappy heels from earlier while Trevor ignored her and watched TV naked. There was a plethora of toys spread out on the bed next to him, and Trevor spoke to him without looking away from the set.

"We've been waiting for you." Then he met Cade's eyes and the two exchanged a look. Cade walked to the bed and removed his clothes on the way, purposely avoiding talking to Riley. He picked up a thin silver chain with two padded clamps on the ends and brought it to Riley. As he ran the cool metal along her neck and exposed breasts, he finally spoke to her. "You've been a bad girl, Riley." He whispered it, his lips against her ear as he spoke, loving the way she jolted and shivered for him.

"Can you guess what this is, Riley?" he asked, brushing the padded tip of the clamp back and forth over one tightly

121

puckered nipple. She shook her head no and whimpered, her hands clenching on the rope that held her captive. "It's a clamp," he said, closing it over the tender bud just as he said it.

Riley jerked and screamed. She had not been expecting that. It hurt the same way that it did when they bit her. It was unending, and she started to pant in an effort to contain the pain. Then without warning, her other nipple was caught. "Ahhh. God. That hurts." Riley bit her lip to try to stop the words, not wanting to beg, afraid that she would before the night was over anyway.

Cade hummed appreciatively at the picture she made with her nipples clamped and the silver chain connecting them swaying as she panted in reaction to the pressure. It would continue to build and throb, and then, when they were ready, the rush of blood filling them when the clamps were removed would be so intense she would probably come from it. Cade smiled at the thought, looking forward to that moment. Trevor stood and tugged gently on the chain, thrilling to her cry of shock. She was hurting, they knew, but she was not asking them to stop. Most importantly, she was not screaming spinach.

Trevor chose a small plug from the bed next. He covered it with lube and stepped behind her. Cade stepped in front of her and reached around to grip a rounded cheek in each hand then he spread her wide for Trevor.

"Oh, baby, you've got the sweetest ass," Trevor said to her as he rubbed the plug in teasing circles around her small back hole. Then, in one steady push, he plunged it in as far as it would go. The scream Riley let out was deep and guttural, and it heated the men's blood to the boiling point. Riley started to shake her head no repeatedly. Her whole body tensed as tight as a bowstring while they held her captive on the razor's edge between pain and pleasure.

Cade picked the next toy. It was a tiny butterfly vibrator. He stepped up to her, smelling the clean sweat that was dewing on her body. Loving the way the corset restricted her breathing, making her gasps whisper soft and fast. He wrapped the strings of the butterfly around her hips and Trevor tied them in back, then Cade positioned the mini vibrator right on her clit. He fed the last string thru the middle of her legs. Trevor tied it to the others, making sure the string was snug up her crack so that when it moved it would bump the plug too. Then Cade turned it on.

Riley screamed again as the tiny bug vibrated with surprising force right against her swollen nub, sending her into an instant climax that made her knees buckle with the force of it. "Oh God. Stop. Please stop." Riley broke. The climax was as intense and as painful as it was exhilarating. She couldn't escape. The vibrator on her clit moved with her as she twisted in an effort to dislodge it, the twisting moved the plug in and out of her stretched ass. It also made the chain on her breasts sway and tug on her sore nipples. Riley had reached her limit and was ready to do anything to stop the feelings.

Trevor kissed her, his tongue filling her mouth at the same time he removed the clamps from her nipples. Riley jolted and screamed into his mouth, coming again and filling Trevor's mouth with her cries of passion as the blood rushed violently back into the tips of her breasts.

The clamps were gone but the plug still stretched her backside and the vibrating on her clit kept her in a constant state of mini orgasms. Both men stepped back from her, and she heard something that sent her blood racing. It sounded like a lot of heavy material and metal, and she didn't have a clue what else they could have in store for her. Then something heavy flopped against her back and jangled as it was attached to what she could only guess was the same swivel clamp in the ceiling that her rope was attached to. Next, something was strapped to her legs; it cupped along the outsides of her hips and cradled high against her back. Her hands were finally let down, but only to be strapped into the same thing that cradled the rest of her. Then Riley remembered Cade mentioning that the first time they took her back hole it was going to be in the hanging chair and a whole new wave of heat swept thru her.

She heard a sound that was similar to a ratchet and felt herself being lifted off her feet. There were tugs at each of her legs and more ratcheting and in far too short a time Riley was hanging from the ceiling with her legs bent and stretched wide until her knees were tucked tight in her armpits and her bottom was exposed and swaying.

"Oh God."

Riley was turned on and frightened at the same time. They had been good to her, had not given her true, pure pain yet, but this was scaring her in a way she wasn't finding pleasing.

The men, recognizing the change in her voice moved in at once. This wasn't going to work if she was truly in pain or really afraid. Ultimately, it was her pleasure that mattered, hers that was the catalyst of this trio.

"Shh," Cade whispered against her lips. "Shh, Riley. You're safe. You're still safe."

Trevor's hands tenderly soothed her sore breasts as he murmured, "It's okay, little one. The clamps are gone, that was your punishment, the rest is all fun from here on out. It's okay."

Cade kissed her eyes over the blindfold tenderly as he repeated, "You're still safe, Riley." The tension eased out of her and she felt the desire swamp her senses again as fast as it had fled. Cade and Trevor sensed it too and stepped back from her. Cade motioned to Trevor and the two switched places and stepped up to her. Cade spoke quietly into her ear as he gripped the plug and rubbed it in bigger and bigger circles, stretching the tight ring of muscles. "I hope you're ready for this. I have been dreaming about it all night." Then he slipped the plug out and nudged his swollen cock in gently until just the bulbous head was buried in her. All the preparation of the last few days had led to this. Her muscles clamped like a vise on him and, taking his control by the teeth, he worked for slow blissful minutes adjusting her to his presence there with small circular nudges that fed his cock in deeper and deeper until he was completely engulfed in her. "Ah, yessss. Baby, God that's tight." Cade's voice was a deep, gravely, growl in her ear. Trevor stepped up in front of her and plunged into her in one slow deep thrust. The way she was hanging kept her legs out of the way and had her hips at the perfect height for them to take her like this since they were roughly the same height, getting into her tight little body was just a matter of bending their knees and straightening up. Riley moaned while her entire body flexed and lunged in her restraints. Cade yelled, his shaft caught in her back hole and being squeezed repeatedly by her clenching muscles. The torment was too much, and Cade withdrew then pushed back in. The lube prevented her muscles from clenching tight enough to slow him down, so he slid right in to the hilt and shouted at the intense pleasure. She was tight and hot. He felt like he was standing in front of a fire. Trevor was also in her to the hilt and each man felt the other thru the thin barrier of skin separating them.

It was an intimacy they had shared before with other women. One that strengthened the bond between them each time, but this time, with Riley, they knew was different. Their eyes locked over her head as the incredible intimacy of the moment irrecoverably fused Riley into their lives and their hearts.

One man bent to each side of her neck, teeth gripping, and then they began to move. One in and the other out so Riley was never without one of them deep inside her.

Her body was consumed with fire. Her flesh stretched until tears filled her eyes and leaked out the corners. Riley had no thoughts, no words, just colors swirling behind her eyelids and the soul wrenching sounds of lust each man made as they took pleasure from her and gave it back tenfold. The tiny butterfly still attached to her clit was vibrating madly and it would multiply with each thrust Trevor made because he would purposely grind against it, knowing the added stimulation was needed to enhance the double penetration. Riley could hardly breathe within the corset and the lightheadedness was just another layer to the madness of feelings storming through her. She felt the next climax coming like a geyser building up and didn't know how to contain it.

"Ohgod!" Then she was bucking and screaming as an endless loop of explosions went off inside her over and over again. Distantly she felt Cade and then Trevor clench and buck as they too succumbed to the pleasure and blasted one hot stream of come into her after another. Their hoarse cries echoed in her ears like a chorus while their bodies twitched and shook as if they'd been shot.

Chapter Thirteen

One week later Riley's mom called to check on her. Riley was on her back on the couch with her head on Trevor's lap. Her soft red cashmere sweater was pulled up around her neck and her breasts were tight and rosy from the teasing that Trevor had been putting them thru while they watched a DVD. The button and zipper were open on her jeans and Trevor currently had one long finger making lazy circles on her clit.

They had just gotten back from a tour of the Statue of Liberty. Cade and Trevor had groaned when she had begged them to take her to see it but in the end they hadn't been able to refuse her. Now Cade was at the club dealing with something that had to do with invoices, and she and Trevor had decided to watch a movie while they waited.

When her cell phone went off in her purse, she jumped startled out of the sexual haze Trevor had been weaving around her. At first, she wanted to ignore it but Trevor told her to answer it with a smile. She reached for it knowing that smile meant he wasn't going to stop, was in fact going to double his efforts and she was going to have to sound as normal as possible while he did.

She fished the phone out of her purse without looking, "Hello?" she said, not knowing if she hoped the call went quick or if she wanted it to last forever. Then the world dropped out from under her and she clamped one hand on Trevor's wrist to try to pull him away. "Hi, Mom." Trevor pinched her clit in retaliation and didn't let up until Riley quit trying to make him stop. "Umm, nothing...just watching a movie."

Trevor slipped his hand out of her jeans and she let out a sigh of relief. Her relief was short lived though because he started tugging her jeans over her hips and off. While she told her mom about the Statue of Liberty, Trevor opened her legs, draping one over the back of the couch and the other out on the floor, leaving her completely open for him. His fingers lightly brushed over her outer lips, tingling and teasing while her mom told her that her dad had put in a new ceiling fan in the living room. She murmured, "Oh really? How's it work?" and then Trevor opened the dewy lips to rub and stroke the inner flesh.

As she was filled in on the latest in family gossip Trevor upped the anti by leaning forward and taking one nipple in his mouth to suck it hard and deep as he plunged two fingers into her. Her hips jerked and lifted, and she fisted her free hand in his hair, not quite managing to stifle her moan.

"What was that, dear?" Trevor heard her mother say and smiled darkly around the breast in his mouth.

"Nothing, Mom." If Riley's reply was too breathy there was nothing she could do about it. "Umm, what was that about Uncle Charlie?"

"Dear?" Riley's mom asked. "Are you feeling alright? You sound funny." Trevor, the brat, chose that moment to flex his fingers and stroke against that spot in her that never failed to make her scream. Thankfully, he wasn't a total monster and stuffed a throw pillow in her face as he did it. She screamed into it instead of her mother's ear. Her mom went on for a while longer and, after making Riley promise to call after her first day in the new branch, she hung up.

Riley dropped her phone and the pillow, then grabbed Trevor by the hair and pulled him up for a biting kiss. She was in a fever pitch thanks to him, and she was going to make him finish what he started. With a gasp and moan, she ripped open his fly and impaled herself on his throbbing shaft. Trevor lunged forward and spread her out on the coffee table, pulling her legs up to drape over his shoulders. He groaned deep in his chest as the position allowed him deeper access than he'd ever had from her, and set a hard, fast rhythm that brought them both to climax in record speed.

Sweating and panting the two of them snuggled in the afterglow. Riley wondered how in the world she had made it her whole life without these two. Her two week trial was almost over and it was time to make a decision. She wondered if she was being selfish wanting to keep them and her job. Did she not trust them? Was the part of her that wanted to quit and fully devote herself to them the selfish part? After all, if she took what they offered she would be the one who got everything. She would be supported. She would be pampered. Her every whim would be met. They had been doing that nonstop for almost two weeks and showed no signs of slowing down. She wanted to see the Met, so they had taken her. She wanted to see Central Park, and the next thing she knew she was in a horse-drawn carriage strolling through it.

They had relented to her cooking for them too. They had both the penthouse and the townhouse stocked and gave her unlimited credit at a delivery market so she could cook to her heart's content for them. Everything she ever wanted was at her fingertips and more.

Sex. Ah lord, the sex. They were insatiable, and she had a

suspicion that she was too. Every touch, every kiss, every look was a whole new layer to the sensual web they had caught her in. There was nothing they had done to her that she would change, or even moderate. She loved how they took command of her. It made her feel possessed, but in good way. They reacted to every nuance of her responses. They learned what made her moan or twitch and exploited that knowledge without mercy— either by bringing her to endless orgasms or by withholding them from her until the torment reduced her to begging. It was amazing and mind blowing. She wished she knew how to eat her cake and have it too.

That night Cade found it impossible to sleep. Someone was stealing from him. After the mix up with the liquor delivery, he had done some discrete digging and cross referencing and had found several discrepancies in everything from liquor to the crystal and china he had imported. Nothing too big. Nothing he wouldn't have chalked up as broken or miscounted merchandise if he'd stumbled across them individually. But together? Together he was looking at thousands of dollars of missing items, and it pissed him off.

He screened every employee carefully before they were hired. He insisted on credit checks and references for everyone he allowed in his employ. In his club, he couldn't be too careful. If a person wasn't above stealing, then they weren't above exposing certain aspects to a reporter or tabloid for the right price. If he didn't find this person or persons soon, it wasn't just his club and his reputation that would be ruined. A lot of people trusted in his ability to keep their secrets safe, and if they became known, a lot of lives would be damaged, some beyond repair. Cade ran a frustrated hand through his hair and stared out at the sparkling city. The solace the view usually brought eluded him.

Riley at first didn't know what woke her. She woke knowing something was wrong. Then she realized what it was. She could breathe. The three of them slept like a pile of puppies in a basket. Sometimes Cade would be on the bottom of the pile and sometimes Trevor, but always she would be squashed in the middle...smothered. So having over six feet of hard male missing from off her back woke her up. She reached a hand to the empty side of the bed and found the sheets cool to the touch, and her heart ached a little. She knew he had been distracted and worried about work when he got home. He had not flirted with her the way he normally did and had only held her close, like a security blanket, instead of the rough and passionate embrace he normally gave her. It saddened her that he was upset. Especially that it was bad enough to keep him from his bed and sleep. As quietly as she could she slipped away from Trevor, hoping that his sleep wouldn't be disturbed and went to find Cade.

He was standing naked in front of the windows. His back was so perfectly formed she marveled at it in awe. Muscles and contours and sleek chiseled lines framed him from neck to toes, covered with smooth dusky skin that she knew tasted like heaven. She tiptoed to him, quiet and soft to lean full length against his hard male flesh. She had dragged on Cade's button up shirt that was heaped on the floor, but she made sure it was not between his back and her front so that they both could wallow in the differences between their bodies as she wrapped her arms around his middle and pulled herself in tight.

"Hi," she kissed softly on the skin between his shoulder blades. "I missed you." Another kiss and a small nibble. She smiled as it raised gooseflesh along his spine.

"Missed me?" Cade's reply was a gruff whisper, slightly distracted, even though he reached one hand back to run affectionately over her hip and buttocks.

"Sure, missed you." Another nibble and a small swipe of her tongue. "I woke up when I realized I could breathe." He chuckled softly like she had hoped he would and tugged on her until she was standing in front of him. When she looked up to his beloved face, she felt something crumble in her chest. She loved him. This intense, demanding, complicated man who was built like an Olympian warrior from Greece. She loved everything about him. The way he hurt over his work, the way it ate at him, showed his dedication and drive. She loved the way he loved Trevor. The two were closer than she had ever known two straight men could be. There was genuine love between them, a love she felt blessed to be a part of. Blessed that they welcomed her to share in that with them.

She couldn't help with whatever was bothering him at work. He was keeping it close to himself. She knew he hated that she hadn't agreed to stay yet. The possibility that she might walk out on them in two days was also a worry weighing on him. That she could help him with. Right now.

"Cade." She gathered all her courage and the love she felt for them both filled her eyes. She wished Trevor were here so she could tell them both, but at the same time, she treasured this moment of just the two of them. She decided when she told Trevor she loved him for the first time, they would be alone too.

Cade looked at her precious face and could not resist reaching a hand up to cradle it. She was so delicate his palm cupped her from chin to temple, his fingers sliding into her messy curls. She had become beloved to them so quickly. Her presence was enough to ease some of the tension that he had dragged around all day. His other hand lifted so he could trace her dainty features one by one, knowing that even if he went blind, he'd be able to know her by feel and taste. He began to dip his head to her lips when she spoke, just a whisper away so her words fluttered across his mouth like butterfly wings. "Cade. I love you. I love you both. If you still want, I'll stay. I'll stay forever if you'll let me."

Chapter Fourteen

The words lanced through him with the precision of a sharpshooter. He felt every muscle in his body bunch and coil with instant arousal. His cock filled painfully, a primitive part of him wanting, no needing, to claim what had become his. His hands that had just been so gentle on her face, gripped hard and he growled deep in his chest as he swooped in to thrust his tongue to the back of her mouth in a kiss as brutal and as consuming as the feelings rushing through his body.

"Mine," he said into her plundered mouth, ripping the open shirt from her shoulders and slamming her against the glass. "Mine," he said again, reaching down and hooking one of her knees in the crook of his elbow so he could plunge into her.

Riley screamed around his kiss at the unexpected invasion, caught off guard in the maelstrom of emotion pouring off him, not having expected her tender declaration to lead to this firestorm of need. She was defenseless against it, her body trained by them to respond to their every touch. In two strokes she was wet and dripping for him. Her body thundered against the window in time to his lunges. He held her leg higher and shifted for his next thrust. Bam! Riley's head fell back on a scream. Bam! He was so deep, so hard. Both their bodies sweat and heaved while they strained together. Bam! Again. Harder.

It wasn't enough. Cade thought. It would never be enough. He braced her shoulders against the glass and grabbed her other leg, holding them wide for him. He pulled his hips back and pounded into her as fast and hard as he could, thrilling to her cries and pants as his body plundered hers until, like an engine at its peak, he broke. The orgasm raked through his groin like a red-hot poker, and his entire body jerked with it as he flooded her womb in a hot pulsating rush. Distantly, he heard her cries as her own orgasm consumed her. It caused her vaginal walls to ripple around his shaft repeatedly, until the sensations were so intense he thought he was going to pass out.

Without his knowledge of how they got there, Cade realized that they were on the floor and Riley was practically bent double under him. He didn't have the strength to carry her to the bed. He did the next best thing and lunged to the side. At least he wasn't squishing her any more. Her legs fell with an undignified plop to the floor and she laid panting and staring at him with a slightly baffled look on her face. He felt that clenching in his chest again, that clenching in his soul. He smiled at her and leaned forward to lay a feather light kiss on her lips. "Thank you, sweetheart. For staying."

Riley wrinkled her nose at him. If he wasn't ready to say the words, that was okay. She could wait. But darned if she was going to say them again till he did. Especially if this was the reaction she was going to get when she did. At least she wasn't going to say it unless they were close to a bed. Ow. Riley felt like she had been pummeled. She gave him a disgruntled look as she reached to her back and tried to rub the base of her spine where she was sure he'd snapped it. Cade chuckled and rolled her until she was face down on his lap as he was braced against the window. Then he started rubbing in deliciously firm circles on her poor abused back. She sighed like a contented kitten

135

and arched into the caresses. She could definitely get used to this.

"Mine," Cade repeated, softer this time, but no less intense.

"Yes," Riley said, turning her head in his lap to smile at him. "Yours." Then her eyes widened, and her body tensed. "I hope we didn't wake up poor Trevor. He was beat tonight."

"Don't worry, Ry," Cade said, touched that she was always thinking about them in small thoughtful ways. "Trev could sleep thru the second coming. We didn't wake him." Riley was not convinced and said as much. "If we woke him, don't you know by now he would have come to join us? He can't resist your sweet little body any more than I can." That made sense to her, but she wasn't going to be happy until they were all back in bed where they belonged so Cade gave in and helped Riley to her feet. The two of them staggered like drunks back to bed and sure enough, Trevor was dead to the world and didn't even flinch when they piled in on top of him. Riley had one last thought as she drifted off to sleep. In case Trevor had a similar reaction to her telling him she loved him, she was going to make sure she told him in bed.

The next morning the boys were speechless as they stared at the meal Riley had prepared for them. She had snuck out of bed before either of them had woken up and they didn't stir until the spicy wonderful smells drifting in from the kitchen had made it impossible for even Trevor to sleep. There was a stack of homemade flour tortillas that made the store bought ones look like cardboard. There were red scrambled eggs that smelled like Mexican nirvana. Riley had called it chorizo and eggs, a dish her daddy used to make for her every Saturday when she was a little girl. The chorizo was a spicy Mexican sausage that she had mixed with beaten eggs, and she'd explained that you didn't eat it with forks. Instead, you had to tear off pieces of tortilla and pinch it up with your fingers. She demonstrated the first bite for each of them, feeding them in turn and got similar reactions from them. They both fell on the food like scavengers and a dozen eggs and fifteen tortillas were gone before she could blink.

They both had to work that day—Cade at the restaurant and Trevor at Flatbush to put some things in order for an upcoming fundraiser. Riley had to go over some things first. Just because she was going to let them keep her, did not mean she was going to stay with the original plan they had laid out for her, and she wanted to get that straightened out now.

"Um, guys," she began, before they headed off to get ready for the day. "I have some things I'd like to talk to you about before we go to work for the day."

"We?" Cade said. She wasn't going anywhere. They had movies for her, and they were taking her to the townhouse. She would be able to soak in the hot tub and ease her body while they were gone. No he didn't like the we at all.

Trevor was frowning at her too. He knew there was something different. It was something in the way Cade kept looking at Riley, something very possessive and almost greedy. He was worried that she might have said something about not staying with them to Cade, and Trevor did not like what that did to his gut. The thought of her thinking about not staying made him almost frantic, and he had insane images in his head of tying her up in the chair and keeping her prisoner until she agreed to stay.

"Umm..." Riley smiled at Cade conspiratorially and placed one hand on his arm in a silent message to wait, then looked Trevor in the eye and felt tears fill her own to flood over. But before she could talk past the lump in her throat, Trevor mistook her intentions and shot to his feet.

"No," he shouted. "No. I mean it. Dammit, Cade." He pointed an angry finger at his best friend, baffled that they, who had always felt the same about everything, could be on such different wavelengths. "What are you thinking? Riley! You are not fucking leaving. Do you hear? You are ours. You're staying and that's it. God." Trevor struggled as he felt panic settling in around his chest and didn't know how to keep it back. He loved her. He did. He knew Cade felt the same, and he could not fathom that she thought they were going to let her walk out the door.

"Shh, Trevor." Riley was frantic to calm him down. If she had any doubts left that they loved her, Trevor's reaction to the thought that she was leaving put those to rest. "Trevor. Listen to me. I'm not going anywhere. That's not what I meant. Just listen. I told Cade last night, and I wanted to tell you now." She smiled into his eyes as he sat and scowled at her, waiting. "I'm staying. I've decided to stay."

The relief wilted Trevor like a deflated balloon. He felt euphoric with it in fact. He reached out with both hands to drag her into his lap to kiss her, feeling the same need to plunder that Cade had the night before. But Riley pushed back and pulled away. She needed to talk and if they started touching her, she would not get a single word in before they had to leave. She scooted away and placed the table between her and the men. That way they couldn't distract her with their hands to try and get their way.

"Now," she began. "Just because I'm staying doesn't mean I'm staying on your terms." She smiled at the twin frowns that got her. "Oh, don't scowl at me. I can't just lie around all day every day for the rest of my life. I need something to do. I was hoping that maybe one of you could give me a job? From what happened last time at the club, I know neither of you would go for me working there."

"Damn right." Both men grumbled, their faces angry at just the thought.

She continued, "What about with you, Trevor? You know I love charity work. Is there something I could do with you, in your organization? That way if you were my boss, you could make sure I was available whenever you two needed me."

Both men were frowning at her. They didn't like her having any responsibility other than themselves.

"C'mon guys. I'm giving you what you want. I love being here, and I love what we have together, but I will shrivel without a purpose that is more than my own little circle of life. I am not the type of person who can be content to spend my days worried about my manicure and the latest fashion. The world is a lot bigger than me and my own problems and I was raised better than that. Just like you two were."

It was just the right button to push, and both men groaned. She had them. They would never be content to live the way they wanted her to, but they weren't happy about it and gave in grudgingly. It took a full hour of arguing and squabbling before all three of them were satisfied. None of them got everything they wanted, but they had reached a compromise that they could live with, and Riley knew that eventually, they would adjust and settle until they were happy. She felt it right down to the bottom of her heart. They were going to be happy, she knew it.

That afternoon Trevor was working on the speech he had to give that weekend at a luncheon. He didn't like public speaking, but he was proficient at it, and he saw it as a necessary evil in his life.

Riley was lounging on the couch in his office, waiting for the day to be done with so they could go home. They were taking her to the theatre tonight to see *Sweet Charity* and she was all but bouncing up and down with impatience. But he wasn't leaving until he got this right. They needed people to dig deep for this new project, and it wasn't going to happen if he couldn't get them motivated.

"Little one," Trevor said without looking up from his notes. "Be still or I'm going to turn you over my knee. I'm trying to concentrate."

Riley could not sit still. This was the best day ever. She and Trevor had worked it out so she could be involved in the new rec center he was starting for girls. Of course, she was only going to be putting in about twenty hours a week if she was lucky, but it was a start. Tonight she was going to see her first ever Broadway play. Things just didn't get any better than this.

She looked at Trevor, so diligent and studious. She smiled and thought he looked a little like Indiana Jones in professor mode, only more hunky. Since her heart felt like it might burst if she didn't let the words out, she got up to lock the door to his office, just in case. He was absorbed in what he was doing. She didn't think he noticed until he looked up at her when she got to his desk.

"What are you up to, Ry?" he asked, a fire already burning in his eyes because he had noticed her lock the door.

"Well,—" she came around to kneel in front of him as he turned in his seat, a puzzled look on his face, "—I told Cade last night, and I wanted to wait until later to tell you, like in bed." She slid one gentle hand up his thigh. "But I can't wait that long." That hand cupped warmly over the growing bulge in his lap, and Trevor sighed and adjusted to give her better access. Riley grabbed tight to his shaft and pulled firmly and quickly to bring herself up and between his spread knees. She stared at him straight in the eye, not two inches from his face and said, "I love you, Trevor. I love you both." Then she bit teasingly at his bottom lip and said, "I just thought you should know."

Everything in Trevor clenched at her words, instantly aroused. Trevor felt a cloak of calm settle over him. He felt the need to dominate, to exert his control and revel in the joy of having Riley give herself completely to him.

"Stand up on my desk," he said, his voice quietly stern and serious. Riley locked her gaze on his and felt a sizzle shoot through her groin at the clear demand in his voice and demeanor. She shakily got to her feet and climbed onto his desk. Her hands trembled at her sides.

Trevor let his gaze roam over her. They had dressed her in a navy blue cashmere sweater and a plaid school girl skirt today with ankle socks and a pair of black and white saddle shoes. Her hair was pulled back and up in a high ponytail; she looked like a school boy's wet dream.

"Unbutton your sweater," Trevor instructed. "Start at the bottom." Slowly, she complied, revealing her olive toned skin inch by inch. "Stop." Trevor said when she had all of them undone but the top one.

"Now. Unhook your bra." She reached to the front clasp and released it, then pulled the cups back until they hung under the open sweater. Her ample breasts were round and high, the beaded crests a dark dusky rose. "Show me your pussy."

She looked at him with wide eyes, not expecting that. If he would have said take off your skirt that would have been one thing. But the way he had phrased it was scandalous to her and it sent a naughty thrill through her body as she tentatively lifted the front of her skirt.

Trevor groaned at the sight before him. Her soft sweater framed those perfect breasts. Her dainty hands held up her childish skirt while she showed him the prettiest little pussy he'd ever seen, the irresistible image rounded out by her feet in her fifties era shoes. She bent one knee as she squeezed her thighs together in an effort to ease some of the ache that was building in her and Trevor smiled at the pleasure he felt knowing that she was enjoying herself as much as he was.

"Widen your stance." She did, placing her feet shoulder width apart. "Keep you skirt up with one hand and spread those pretty pussy lips with the other," he ordered in a harsh sex-raspy voice. When she hesitated he commanded, "Do it now and don't hesitate again to do what you're told, or I will spank you." She sucked in a shaky breath and slipped a gentle hand to her moistening flesh. Her fingernails were painted a deep red, and they pushed between the folds and opened the lips to reveal the tiny nub and glistening opening of her sheath. Her fingers making a red tipped vee, framing her delights for him.

"Good. Now stay there." Then he picked up his speech and went back to work.

Riley stared in open-mouthed shock. She couldn't believe he was going to leave her like this. Every part of her was on display for him, she was standing on his desk like an X-rated paperweight, and he was working on his speech. She was so turned on she was sure that just one touch on her clit and she would come, but he blithely went back to work. It was maddening. It was torture. And, it was exhilarating. There was something delicious about being on display like this and yet ignored. It made her feel like a sex slave from some bygone era, and her body was thrumming in impatience to see this through.

Trevor was staring intently at the papers in his hand, but for all he comprehended, they could be written in Greek. He could smell her arousal, with his peripheral vision he could see how she trembled with desire for him to continue. He knew that the longer he could hold back the better it would be for both of them, and it was a wonderful torment.

After what seemed like an hour, he gathered his speech in one hand and stood. Without looking at her, he reached his other hand out to her exposed pussy. His blunt fingers slipped over and around her weeping flesh, circling the clit and opening. Flicking and tugging on the lips that she held back for him, dipping into the clenching depths while he read the finished speech.

Riley's knees buckled, and she started to come. "Stop." Trevor's voice was dark and commanding, and he pinched painfully on one of her labia making her squeak. "You will not come. Not until you've heard my speech. Do you hear? Not until I'm done. If you try to come before that I'll pinch you again, and if you do let yourself come, I'll turn you over my knee and spank your sweet little ass until you can't sit down." He looked up at her then and the fire blazing in his eyes was enough to make her whimper. "Understand, little one?"

"Ye-Yes," Riley stammered, trying hard to concentrate on anything but his hand between her legs. She was afraid she wouldn't be able to hold back the orgasm no matter the consequence. He nodded approval at her compliance and started fondling her again. His fingers were wide and had calluses on them from his constant labor. They felt like heaven on her tender flesh, and the way he moved them on her was glorious. Riley felt her climax coming closer and tried clenching all her muscles to hold it back. Trevor was reading on and without a break in his speech, he again pinched one of her lips. Riley yelled, the pinch painful enough to push back the pending explosion, but in a way also bringing her to an even higher level of arousal. Of their own accord, her hips started flexing and dipping, riding the fingers that were dipping in and out of her.

Trevor kept reading, but even though his voice was calm and monotone, his entire focus was on Riley and her luscious body. His whole hand was coated with her juice. His head was filled with the scent of her. He pulled his fingers out of her, then traced the fingers that were holding her spread open for him, and he used his thumb and middle finger to swirl and lightly pluck at her clit. It was swollen with need, and he wanted nothing more than to suckle on that little bit of flesh, but he had set the rules for this game. He wasn't going to break them. He went on talking about reformed kids and the drop of crime in this district since the rec center while he took three fingers and rubbed them rapidly over her clit, pushing hard and fast against it as Riley panted and yelped, biting on her lip in an effort to hold back her climax.

He could tell she was going to break, so he pulled his hand away and walked to the other side of his desk, behind her while his voice grew in volume and passion as the speech got to the part about the importance of nurturing the children of this country. From behind her Trevor instructed, "Bend over and grab your ankles." At first she didn't respond, so far gone she didn't comprehend that he was speaking to her and not just reading from his speech. He had to repeat himself and give a sharp slap to her bottom.

When she did as she was told, he lifted her skirt and draped it over her back, exposing all her secrets to him to do with as he wished. He slid his hand between the rounded cheeks of her ass and pushed his thumb into the rosebud of her back hole. He pumped in and out, smooth and slow three times, then pushed his middle finger into her pulsating slit.

Riley shot to her toes and yelled out a plea. "Oh, Trev. Oh please. Please, I'm going to come. I'm going to come." She was senseless with her begging. "Please. Please let me come."

Trevor leaned forward and bit her on the ass, hard. "No." Riley yelped, the pain another layer to the madness he was building in her. Soon, she knew she wouldn't be able to stop, and she resigned herself to a spanking.

"Well. What have we here?" Cade's voice was smooth and amused from just inside the doorway. Riley squeaked in shock and tried to straighten up. Trevor stopped her by pinching the fingers in her ass and pussy together, the pain immediately getting her compliance. She again grabbed her ankles and resolved herself to whatever they wanted to do to her. "How did you get in? The door was locked."

Cade came around to the front of Trevor's desk and bent forward to meet her eyes, "I have a key." He smiled at her and kissed her forehead, acting as if he came upon a sight like this every day.

Trevor then continued his speech, and his fingers continued their torment. Cade sat down in Trevor's chair, steepled his hands and braced his chin on them while he watched. He reached out briefly to tuck her skirt into her waistband so he could have a clear view and then resumed his posture, watching as Trevor tortured her until she was again mindless and begging for him to let her come.

Trevor smacked her butt with his papers and said, "Cade, she's too noisy. It's distracting me. Care to do something about that?"

"My pleasure," Cade said and stood to unbuckle his slacks, pulling his fully erect shaft out. The position put Riley's head at waist level for him, the angle was a little awkward, but she was so turned on she didn't care and just latched her mouth onto his cock and sucked like her life depended on it.

Cade hissed between his teeth and grabbed her by her ponytail. "Jeez, sweetheart," he said between clenched teeth, "God, that's good, baby. Suck it. Yeah, like that. Ah, I love your mouth."

He pumped in hard and fast to the back of her throat. Riley's whole body thrilled to his words and the hot tube of flesh throbbing in her mouth. It was too much and she didn't know how much longer she could hold back. Then the miracle she had been hoping for happened. Trevor finished and set his papers on the desk. Riley whimpered in relief and trembled as she waited for permission to come finally.

Trevor kept his hand buried in her two holes and leaned around her hip to watch Cade pumping in and out of her mouth.

"Ry? Would you like to come now? Huh, baby?" he asked as he changed his rhythm and added his other hand to slide against her clit. She hummed an agreement and nodded around Cade's shaft. "Okay, baby. Okay. Come for us. Come...now." He groaned as her muscles clenched around his fingers, and her garbled screams filled the room while the climax gushed from her body with the force of a tidal wave. Trevor bit the under curve of one luscious cheek, wanting to devour her from head to foot, he was so turned on at the endless waves rippling from her inner muscles he felt close to the edge himself.

"Trev?" Cade cut in, holding back his own release by the teeth. "You got any lube here?" He looked down at her lovely mouth still sucking greedily on his cock and then across her back to where his best friend continued to finger fuck her ass and pussy. "I think it's about time you had a taste of what it's like to be in that sweet ass of hers."

Riley's knees buckled, and she moaned out her eagerness on his shaft. She had loved having them both in her the last time. It had hurt, a lot at first. But it was a delicious hurt, one she had wanted to push into and relish. It had felt so good to have them both in her, so full. Right now she was so turned on she would let them do anything to her, anything as long as they just didn't stop.

"I think she likes that idea," Cade said and gave a sharp tug on her hair, making her eyes sting. "Don't you Ry? You like being full of us, don't you? One in each hole, fucking you till you scream." He chuckled darkly when she moaned out her agreement and nodded again.

"Check the right hand drawer," Trevor said. "I think I have some in there that I keep for emergencies." Cade opened the drawer and brought out a tube to hold in front of Riley. She mewled and blinked at him, scared and exhilarated at the same time.

"Cade," Trevor began, "pull out and go sit on the bench." Cade did, and Riley watched him walk away, her mouth feeling empty without him. He sat on a black leather recliner bench—a fancy lounge chair without armrests. He sat with his legs together in a semi-reclining position and looked expectantly at the two of them, obviously letting Trevor call the shots. Trevor's hand was still pumping in and out of her and he started working his thumb in big circles in her ass, widening the hole for his cock. Riley panted and tried to relax her muscles.

"Riley, straddle Cade and put his cock in this hot little pussy. Keep your knees on the bench and lean forward." She slowly straightened, and he helped her down from the desk.

As soon as she was standing, Cade gave a rumble of approval for her appearance, with her girlish skirt rucked up showing her bare flesh and her sweater opened to frame those tits of hers, it was a delectable sight and he couldn't wait for what was about to come.

Trevor watched her walk to Cade and place herself over and then onto his friend's shaft. It was an arousing sight and he quickly shed his slacks and headed over. "Riley," he said, handing her the lube, "get my dick ready to fuck your ass." The words were purposely crude. He knew that the dirty talk thrilled her as much as everything else that they were doing. He sucked in a harsh breath as she wrapped her hand around his flesh and squirted a generous amount of lube onto it. Her hand stroked and rubbed, covering him from base to tip in a thick slippery layer. She dragged her thumb over the slit on the head, and Trevor groaned at the sensation. He pulled back and stepped behind her, straddling the bench.

He placed his hand on the small of her back and pushed until she was leaning against Cade and her ass was offered up to him like a sacrifice. He placed the tip of the tube on her tightly gathered bud and squeezed, filling the crack. He tossed the tube aside and used his thumb again on her hole, making sure it was well lubed for him. "Get ready, babe." He placed the purpled bulbous head against her, gently pushing back and forth in small nudges until the head slipped in. Her whole body tensed as she tried to pull away from the pain of his intrusion. "Shhh." He groaned, "Ah God, sweetie, don't move. Don't move. I'm on the edge, and I don't want to come yet. Ah God. Cade." He met Cade's gaze over her shoulder. "So fucking good....yeah." He pushed all the way in. Thrilling to her grunting yell as she adjusted to the feel of them both inside her. He pulled back until just his head was in and then with another deep guttural groan, he lunged back in to the hilt.

He shifted and pushed, grabbing a handful of ass in each

hand and spreading her cheeks wide until he was buried as far inside her as he could get. His balls were flush to Cade's and the two of them felt each other thru the thin layer of skin separating them. The moment was so intense and intimate that Trevor felt like the slightest movement would send him over the edge. He took two deep cleansing breaths, latched onto his control by a thread and nodded to Cade. Then Cade flexed and pulled out, then back in and Trevor pulled out, and back and forth it went. Slow and deep, grinding in as far as they could get with each demanding thrust.

Riley was paralyzed between them. Trapped by the two enormous shafts impaling her, by the two six foot plus male bodies commanding her. It was mind blowing and exotic and with their hands gripping and shifting her 'til she was just where they wanted her; it was a moment that blazed in fire across her closed eyelids and she screamed, "I'm coming. I'm coming, oh please. I'm coming."

That was it. Her cries, her clenching inner muscles, snapped the control that they had been clinging to. Both started a furious pounding into her that made her orgasm detonate as they plunged and pounded into her pulsating flesh.

Riley screamed again as she felt the hot shooting jets of Trevor's come when he lunged one last time, balls-deep into her ass. Then Cade, as he came too, pulsing and shuddering deep into her writhing sheath. It was too much, too, too much and Riley shouted again and again as they emptied into her. She felt flooded with their hot come, it filled her and was such an exquisite sensation that Riley didn't know if she could survive it. She bit hard into Cade's chest, unable to stand it anymore, and his shout and growl was a dark reward that thrilled her. He fisted his hand around her ponytail and pulled hard until she released her bite. He brought her mouth up to his to fill with his tongue and then, finally, the incredible tremors at last started to ebb from the three of them.

Trevor collapsed on top of them, sated. He didn't care if he was squishing them. He didn't think he'd be able to move for a week.

Chapter Fifteen

That night after the play, Riley was up to her chin in bubbles. The play was much more than she could have hoped for. It was an experience that was larger than life, and she had been instantly addicted. She had pleaded with huge liquid eyes as soon as they left the theater, and did not stop until they promised to take her again next week.

Now they were back in the penthouse, and Riley was soaking in a bubble bath while they fed her *crème brûlée* and champagne. When they had gotten home and saw the stiffness with which she moved, Trevor had rushed to the bathroom and started the tub while Cade had asked her if she wanted dessert. He'd called and ordered it for her, shocked when she had said she'd never had it before.

Now, she wallowed in the pampering of her two men and purred her contentment as Cade fed her bites of the creamy stuff and Trevor rubbed her bubble coated feet. She didn't have the heart to tell them that she didn't like the dessert. It was good at first, but it had a funny taste that didn't seem to belong with the other flavors in it. The cook in her wondered what it was and why someone had not figured it out and removed whatever it was that was ruining an otherwise delicious dessert. But oh well, she thought, maybe it was like caviar and only rich people liked it. Everything else about this day had been perfect and she wasn't going to let a little after taste bother her.

Fifteen minutes after her bath, Riley was feeling queasy. Her face felt numb, and her stomach was roiling in a greasy, rumbling boil. She was snuggled naked between them and decided that she probably ate too much and just had an upset tummy. Or maybe she drank too much because her limbs felt heavy and her thoughts were foggy. She pushed herself off the couch and shuffled off toward the bed quietly. She did not want the boys to worry, sure it was the mix of champagne and sweets that wasn't settling. She left them watching a late night program and hoped that she could just fall asleep quickly to escape the sickness filling her entire body with surprising speed.

She didn't make it to the bed. Halfway down the hall, something sharp and vicious stabbed thru her side like a knife, and it crumbled her to her knees with a cry. She was in such pain and misery that she only vaguely heard the boys shout as they vaulted from the couch and barreled toward her. They bent over her with worried faces and gentle hands. It was the last clear image she had.

Cade had never felt panic the way he had when she'd cried out. He was basking in the day and all the joy they had shared. Gloating even, in the fact that she loved them and wanted to stay. It was a fairytale for them, and he felt like a damn prancing rooster—he was so high on his good fortune of finding her.

Then, in a split second, it had shattered with her cry of pain. He and Trev had been frozen for an endless second at the sound, and then when they heard her body thump to the floor they galvanized into action. He'd vaulted over the coffee table from his sitting position and reached her in a few long strides, Trevor right at his side.

The sight of her curled in a little ball of agony ripped through his gut with unbearable helplessness. She was covered in sweat and quaking while cramps clenched her body and brought pitiful sounds of anguish from between lips that had turned an alarming blue. Trevor and he locked eyes over her and both recognized the terror in the other. Trevor raced for a phone while Cade tried to get her to speak to him, thinking that if she were talking then that would mean she was going to be okay. But she couldn't answer, or even shake her head in response to his questions.

Trevor dialed 911 on his cell and raced back to Riley. Her lips and chin were blue, and her breathing was getting alarmingly raspy. It took three rings for the phone to be picked up but it seemed like thirty to him. "I need an ambulance, fast," Trevor said after the operator answered, he gave the address to the penthouse and snarled at the operator for suggesting that he calm down and tell her what was the nature of the emergency. "It's our girlfriend. She collapsed. Her face is turning blue, and she won't talk to us."

"Is she breathing, sir?" the frustratingly calm voice asked.

"Yes, but it's raspy, not very deep."

"Can you check her pulse for me? Do you know how?" she asked. He did and found it feather light and way too fast. Then he swore and dropped the phone when Riley's eyes rolled back in her head, and she started convulsing. Her tiny little body shook as if it was in the jaws of an invisible dog, and both men felt bone deep fear that they might be losing her right before their eyes.

"Sir? Sir? You have to listen to me. Sir?" Trevor only dimly heard the voice from the phone as he and Cade tried to hold Riley down thru the spasms, but he grabbed for the phone, hoping she would tell him something to do that would help.

"I'm here. I'm here. She convulsing, and now I don't think she's breathing anymore. Oh God! Help her. Please." He had no idea that tears were spilling down his cheeks as she flopped back and her mouth worked without any air or sound coming from it. Her face was ghost white. He thought if they didn't do something soon, they would lose her. The operator told him to check her mouth for obstructions. He relayed it to Cade. Cade cradled her head back, opened her mouth and swept his finger in.

"There's nothing in there," Cade told him, tears of his own leaking unheeded from his eyes. "I don't think anything's blocking her breathing." He followed instructions and opened her mouth as wide as it would go and pushed on her tongue. A tiny gasp could be heard. At least some air was going in and out. Then Cade was instructed to hold her nose and give her two deep puffs. As he did, she was caught again in the grip of convulsions, and her violent jerking cut his lip on her teeth. He didn't feel the pain, even as blood flowed freely from the split. He sat back and watched, helpless, as she writhed. Her body bowed backwards at an impossible angle until they heard joints popping, and he thought the spasm was going to crack her spine.

After what seemed like hours, the paramedics were there, and Cade ran to open the elevator and let them in. Before they knew it, she was strapped to a gurney with tubes in her arm and a bag on her face, while a medic asked them what drugs they'd given her.

"What?" Cade growled at the man, affronted.

"Look," the medic continued, apparently unfazed by his bravado, "if you don't tell me what she's on, she'll die. I'm not the cops, and even if I were, are you willing to let her die over this?" he said, pumping the bag.

Cade fisted his hands at his side and fought the urge to pound them into him. He knew the man was trying to help. If he killed him, it would take time away from helping Riley.

"We don't do drugs, man," Trevor broke in, a dead calm icing his veins with dread. "We sure as hell wouldn't drug our girlfriend. Do whatever you have to do and fix her." Before the tech could respond, she convulsed again and her body thrashed hard enough that it almost flipped the gurney that she was strapped to.

They were moving as they talked. They had reached the outside of the building when the other tech said, "Shit. She flat lined." He jumped onto the gurney and began to perform CPR on Riley.

Cade and Trevor froze in helpless panic. Gripping onto each other's hands they watched for four endless minutes as the two medics worked to bring Riley back from the dead. Cade rushed to her despite the medics and whispered furiously in her ear. "You come back. You hear me. Now, or I swear to God, baby, I'll hunt you down and drag you home by your hair." The last of this was a garbled mess as he felt everything in him crumble at the thought that she was truly going to leave them. The desperation was blinding him. Trevor was on his knees, praying while tears silently ran down his face as they worked tirelessly on her poor little body.

The medic with the bag shouted at Cade, "Get over here and pump this. Watch me. Do it just like this. Understand?

Don't stop." As soon as Cade did what he'd ordered, he shoved the gurney to the ambulance while the second medic stayed crouched above her and kept her heart beating. Then he grabbed the paddles and charged them. He yelled for them to move. "Clear." When Cade didn't move he shouted again and the other tech pushed Cade's hands and the bag back. The two paddles were placed on her, one in the middle of her chest and one on her side. *ZAP.* Her body bucked and strained against her restraints, and Trevor shouted out a curse from the door of the ambulance. *Zap.* "Bag," he ordered, and the other tech took the bag from Cade and started pumping again.

One of them placed his scope on her chest and waited. Then, "I got a pulse!" Cade collapsed to the side of the ambulance while Trevor crumbled to the pavement. Then the medics barked out an order and the two scrambled in. Finally, they were flying down the dark streets of New York, sirens blaring and lights flashing while the woman they loved clung to life by a thread.

Chapter Sixteen

At the hospital, they were told to wait outside. It didn't go well when they first tried to take her away. A large no nonsense nurse informed them that they could wait in the waiting room or at the county jail. It made no difference to her. The wait was an intolerable torture to them. Trevor took over the mundane paperwork that seemed a cruel exercise to him at a time like this. But he made sure that her bills would be covered without question. They sat side by side for a while, wordless, pressing into each other's side to draw on and give what support they could to each other. It didn't take long for them to be up and pacing like caged tigers, snarling and growling at any medical personnel who come by without information for them.

A young, harried looking doctor in wrinkled scrubs stopped at the entrance. "Gentlemen? I'm Doctor Baylor. Are you the two who came in with Riley? She's been revived. It was a close call there for a while. But after the blood work revealed that it was heroin we were able to administer an antagonistic to counteract the drug and bring her back from the brink."

Trevor couldn't fathom what he was hearing. There was an almost euphoric rush of relief at hearing that she was revived, followed by the fresh horror that she had been drugged. An angry confusion was building in him and it was a dangerous mix indeed.

Trevor held up a hand and asked, "Can we see her? Is she awake?"

"We have her sedated now," the doctor answered. "Her body's suffered a lot of trauma tonight and it needs the rest. We're going to keep her overnight to run tests on her liver and kidneys. We want to make sure there hasn't been any damage to those organs before we let her go. But yes you can see her as soon as she gets transferred to her room."

Cade grabbed the man's arm, needing to look him in the eye when he asked his next question. "You're sure it was heroin?"

"There is no doubt."

"Were you able to tell how it was given to her?" Cade asked, a terrible suspicion growing in him.

"Orally, from what we could gather. It's the reason I think we were able to save her actually. The body dilutes a large portion of it when taken that way, which is why addicts prefer to shoot it. If she had been injected, we wouldn't have been able to save her." He stopped and took a good look at Cade. "That's a pretty bad cut. Let's go back here, and I'll stitch it up." He reached out, his thumb pulled on the side of the split and he whistled at the depth of the gash. "Don't argue with me. That is not going to heal without a few stitches. C'mon."

Cade and Trevor followed. Cade thinking about the only thing that Riley had eaten that he and Trev hadn't.

"I think it's time you tell me about what's been bothering you so much at work," Trevor said. The two locked eyes over the doctor's head and a silent message passed between them. Someone was going to pay and pay with his or her life if they had any say in the matter.

It took three stitches to close Cade's lip and when it was done they were finally directed to Riley's room. She was pale as the sheets that surrounded her, a tube still in her arm. She had a band on one arm that periodically checked her vitals and there were the unsettling sounds of machines beeping and whirring in the room. Both of them stood frozen in the doorway, waiting for their brains to process the sight before them.

Trevor felt shaken to his core at how close they'd come to losing her. He couldn't help but flash back to the first time he'd seen her. She'd been hidden under the comforter, curled against Cade and as he'd come to her side of the bed the anticipation he'd felt was heady. When Cade had revealed her to him, she'd taken his breath away. If he had been allowed to pick out each body part and facial feature, she would've looked exactly as she did. Then those beautiful eyes had opened, and he hadn't been the same since. Her lovely spirit and fiercely loyal heart, her sense of humor and the way she cried at sappy stuff all combined to make her the one woman that they could not live without.

Now, he tried to accept the sight of her here, attached to wires, pale and bruised and back from the dead, literally. Trevor didn't know he had it in him to feel this deeply. He only knew that if there were doubts about them before, they were now abolished and nothing was ever going to take her from them. Nothing.

Cade felt an ice-cold fury settle in his veins. He spoke to Trevor in a hushed voice so he didn't wake her as he walked to her bedside and gently took her hand.

"Someone has been stealing from the club and restaurant. I stumbled onto it by sheer luck a couple of days ago. I'm sure this was meant for me. The son of a bitch better be in fucking Afghanistan by now, or I'm going to kill him."

"Fuck," Trevor said. He looked as disturbed at the thought that someone had tried to kill Cade as he was that Riley had gotten hurt. "Do you know who did this? Any guess?"

"Not a fucking clue," Cade answered. "I have been quietly going back through the invoices and trying to see if there is a pattern to the thefts and the person signing. I can't find one. Some of the thefts have shown up during inventory checks and not deliveries. There hasn't been one employee who's shown up more than any other has. It's a fucking mess." Cade ran a tired hand thru his hair as the last of his energy drained from him.

The night had been an emotional one, and he didn't think he had the energy left to do anything more than listen to the reassuring sounds of Riley breathing in and out. Trevor slouched in the chair on the other side of Riley and seemed to be in the same shape as he. They would deal with finding the bastard tomorrow, for now it was enough that she was alive. For now, that was all that mattered.

It was early in the morning when the nurse came in to wake Riley. They had been doing it regularly all through the night, but she had been under the influence of the medications and had only been vaguely aware. This time however, her groggy mind fought to clear itself and comprehend what was going on. The first thing she noticed was the painful state of her body. She felt as though she had been beaten bloody, and wondered if she'd been in a car wreck. A pitiful moan garbled out from between her cracked lips, shocking her with its raspiness. She couldn't remember ever sounding like this before.

The next thing she became aware of was that she was in a hospital and there was a nurse hovering over her. The woman had a kind if somewhat distracted manner as she checked tubes and machines and told Riley it was time to wake up and try to go to the bathroom.

"Huh?" Riley looked around painfully, surprised at how much energy it cost her to turn her head. "Wha...happ'n?" Her mouth couldn't get around the words she was trying to say and her heart monitor sped up as fear crept its way into her.

"Hey, babe." The welcome and familiar presence of Cade at her side helped ease her panic. "Shhh...we're here. You're going to be fine, sweetheart." He looked terrible to Riley, his face was pale, drawn and covered in stubble. He looked like he'd been up all night.

"What happened?" She wrinkled her brow and tried to reach out to his swollen, bandaged lip.

"Nothing to worry about, sugar," Trevor said from the other side of the bed. He stepped close, and Riley saw he looked just as shot as Cade. "He was too good looking anyway. Besides, knowing his luck it'll only make him look better."

"Step back, guys," the nurse instructed as she lowered a bed rail. The whole hospital was swimming with speculation about this threesome. To her, there was no way she believed that these men would have drugged this girl. Maybe she was a softie, but men who were as frantic and worried as these two would not have put her in danger in the first place.

It was titillating and decadent to her that they both claimed to be her boyfriend, and if she were honest with herself, all she felt about that was envy...aside from ending up in the hospital. She thought this was one lucky girl indeed.

"C'mon, honey. Let me help you up and that way you can go pee."

Riley whimpered as she was helped to a sitting position and both men's faces tightened at the sound. They looked as if her pain affected them. Riley became determined that she was not going to make another sound. She was not going to be a whiner and watch them sweat over her discomfort.

One painful step after another, Riley made it to the restroom with the nurse's arm around her. Her head felt stuffed with cotton, and her body was throbbing like a sore tooth. There was an enormous pain in her chest and as she sat on the toilet she pulled the gown away to see what was wrong. For the life of her, she could not think of any explanation for the grotesque bruising and circular sores on her chest. She pulled herself up to the sink and washed her face, taking time to rinse her mouth out a couple of times as well. She felt marginally better and hoped that it was a sign that soon everything else would get better too.

When she got back into bed, the doctor came in and smiled.

"Hi, Riley." He said it with so much cheer that she wanted to punch him. She was feeling too miserable to understand why he could be so happy. "You probably don't remember me. You were pretty much out of it last night. I'm Dr. Baylor; I worked on you when you came in. Do you remember anything?"

"No, nothing." Both men had taken up a single side of her bed to make room for the doctor. They each had a hand on her.

"Riley, you were brought in and treated last night for a heroin overdose. You almost died. I have to ask...do you know how the drug got into your system? Did you take it with knowledge or consent?"

"I-I don't. Never. Please, believe me." She looked in panic and pleading, not at the doctor but at her men, afraid they would think she was a user and want her to leave. "I've never,

never done drugs. Are you sure, Doctor? Maybe there's a mistake." Tears leaked from her eyes.

"We believe you. Nobody thinks this was your doing. Do you have any idea who would want to hurt you?"

"No," she said and clung to Trevor and Cade's hands as though she were afraid the doctor was going to take them away regardless of what she said. "No. I just moved here, and I don't know anybody yet. Trevor and Cade would cut off their arms before they'd let me get hurt, so you can stop thinking what I think you're thinking."

Dr. Baylor smiled. "Well, you ingested a lethal amount of pure heroin and it had to get into you somehow. Can you think over what you ate and drank yesterday?"

"We know where it came from," Cade said drawing the attention of the doctor and Riley. Trevor already knew this and just kept his gaze on Riley.

"It was the *crème brûlée* she had last night. We've already called the police and had a detective pick up the dish from the penthouse. It tested positive." When the doctor started to interject, Cade continued handing him one of his business cards with information written on the back. "I wrote down the detective's name and number, he's going to be contacting you about this."

"Okay. Riley, we've run some tests and everything looks like you are going to be just fine. I have ordered some pain meds that should last you till the soreness wears off, a couple of days I'd think. I'll let these two take you home and tell you to have yourself checked by your regular doctor in a week or so. Until then, plenty of bed rest and no alcohol, all right?"

Riley gave her assent and tried not to think about the fact that someone had tried to kill her. It was surreal, and she was sure that as soon as the shock wore off she would be panicking.

Until then she would gladly hide behind the buffer that the shock gave her and allow the boys to take over and get her home.

Chapter Seventeen

She took a pain pill right before she was released, so the ride home and the rest of that first night was a blur to her. She knew that she was cosseted and cared for and that every time she stirred one or both of them were there, hovering.

It was soothing. It was comforting.

After a week, it was driving her nuts.

She was fine. She had no lasting damage, no lingering pains and had in fact secretly stopped taking the pain meds after the first day. Riley knew Cade and Trevor had been scared out of their minds, she tried to understand that and be charmed when they would not let her even walk across the room without hovering, but the charm wore off on that real quick. She'd had a follow up appointment with their family doctor, and he had assured the guys that she was free to resume any and all activities. Nevertheless, they still cosseted her, and she was ready to scream out of pure boredom.

Riley figured she had put it off long enough and called her mom. She felt that her mom had a right to know about these major events that had been happening in her life. It was a tense call.

"Mom, I promise you that you don't have to worry. I'm fine. It was food poisoning, that's all." Since technically it was poisoned food that she suffered from, Riley did not feel she was lying.

"I know, sweets," her mother said in a dire tone that Riley recognized all too well. "It's the rest of what you're telling me that I'm worried about. You want me to believe that my baby has two, two boyfriends and that it's okay?" Riley trusted her mom, knew that she was an open and fair person. If Mom wasn't thrilled, that was fine, but she did expect her mom to let her make her own choices and love her anyway.

"You quit your job, Riley." There was frustration in her voice, and Riley felt truly sorry to have upset her mother that much. "That job is what brought you to the city. That job is why your father and I were okay with you moving so far away. You had a future and security. Now, what have you got?"

"I told you. I have a great job working with inner city kids at a rec center. I'll be doing what I love all the time instead of splitting my time at the bank." Riley thought it best to leave out the part about her boss being one of her boyfriends. She didn't think her mother trusted her judgment that much.

"But honey," her mother beseeched. "You let your apartment go? Really? Your job, your apartment and two boyfriends? You're killing me all in one phone call here. Would you consider coming home? Just for us to see for ourselves that you're okay?"

"Look, Mom," Riley hedged, not knowing what to say. "I don't know when I can get away. I've just started a new job, I haven't got enough saved for a ticket home, you know that, and... I just don't think it's the best time right now."

Cade was on the bed next to her, had listened without a shred of apology to the entire conversation, and put his hand over the mouthpiece. "Tell her we'll be there next Friday." When Riley tried to shake her head no and pull away, he just repeated himself and gave her a look that told her he'd not take no for an answer.

"Umm, I guess, if you really want us to, we'll be there next Friday." Riley was flabbergasted. He had no idea what he'd just voluntarily put himself and Trevor into the middle of. But if he wanted to face the firing squad, it was his funeral.

"We, hmm?" Gail wasn't sure if she was happy or not about the men joining Riley. On one hand with them coming, she would be able to judge for herself what type of men these were. On the other, she was afraid what it meant that they were not letting her come alone. Well, she determined that if she got one inkling that they were mistreating her baby in any way at all, well, they were going back home alone and that was that.

"Well. I hope you're satisfied," Riley said as she hung up the phone. "My parents are going to eat us alive. It would really be better if we put this off till they have like, I don't know, a year to adjust to this before they see you guys." She gave him big hopeful eyes and ground her teeth in frustration when he just chuckled.

"Riley," he said. "We'll see them next weekend, face it and set their minds at ease. They'll see that we adore you and you us and that will be the end of it."

Riley harrumphed and crossed her arms over her chest. "A fat lot you know." This was so going to suck. She did not know how she was going to face her parents with them knowing what she did with these two.

"Hey, Ry, why are you blushing?" Trevor asked as he came in the room.

"Ask Cade," she said with a frustrated grunt and pulled the covers over her head. How was she ever going to be able to look her father in the eye again?

Cade chuckled, amused at her embarrassment. "Her

parents are worried; we're going to visit them next weekend so we can set their minds at ease." Cade had stopped being uncomfortable about his lifestyle choice years ago. If both his and Trevor's families had hoped that the two of them would outgrow their preferences, they did not voice those thoughts aloud. Cade was sure in fact that their parents would come to accept the three of them without reservation. After all, parents only wanted what was best for their children right? For them to be happy. Well, this is what made them happy and what was best for them, with time, they would see that. Cade had no doubts.

"Sounds great. We can look for a place of our own while we're there," Trevor said as he bounced into bed on the other side of Riley. The comment got her to poke her head above the covers, her eyes as big as saucers.

"What do you mean?" she asked in a whisper.

"Well, your family is up there, Ry," Trevor explained. "That means we are going to be making regular trips there. It only makes sense to get a place of our own." He leaned down until they were nose to nose. "You make too much noise for us to stay with them when we visit." He swiped his tongue across her lips. "Unless you want us to gag you every time while we're there?"

Riley supposed she should be prepared for things like this, but she wasn't. Even with all they'd done for her to show her they were serious about keeping her, this newest sign that they were not letting her go was enough to have her heart filling with warmth and things lower getting full and heavy with desire. Her eyelids lowered and her cheeks flushed as she shifted to mesh her lips with Trevor's while a sigh trembled out of her.

As her luscious mouth melded and licked at his, Trevor

groaned and tried to pull back. Riley sensed his intention and she slipped one arm around his neck and clung like a barnacle.

"Riley...mmm... Ry, sweetheart...mmm no. Stop that, ugh. Cade, help." Trevor found it impossible to make himself pull away from her. Her mouth was doing amazing things to his and she was naked under those blankets and every shift she made tugged them lower and revealed more of her sweet flesh. They had denied themselves for a week, keeping their lusts in check and the restraint was torture to them.

Torture to have her this close. Close enough to see and smell and touch, but not take. Now, here she was clinging. Begging for it to end and Trevor didn't think he had what it would take to stop. He looked up from Riley's eager sweet face to beseech Cade to intervene only to see that Cade too was beyond the ability to resist any more. He was kissing and licking his way down Riley's back. Taking sucking nips as he worked his way down to the twin moons of her rear. Trevor watched as Cade grabbed each cheek in turn and took a big suckling bite of each one before spreading them and running his tongue in a wet hot line down her crease. Riley's soft sighs turned to breathless moans by this time, and she groaned deep and hard into his mouth when Cade stiffened his tongue and pushed it into the puckered ring of muscles there.

The sight incited him into action, and he pulled out of Riley's embrace to bury his face in the soft folds of her other lips. Drinking in her essence, lapping at her soft clit while Cade continued to tongue her ass. They shoved Riley's legs up until they were tucked under her chin and her treasures were open and free.

Riley was lost to the sensations that were rioting through

her body. Cade was doing something to her ass that was making it hard not to scream, and Trevor was sucking on her clit with deep surges that were making her head swim. Her body felt alive and on fire in a way it hadn't for the whole week. She held back her orgasm, wanting to drag out the delicious feelings for as long as she could. Then Cade climbed up to his knees and reached for the bedside drawer while he used first one finger then two in her back hole. Even before she felt the cool lube squeeze into her, she knew what was coming and her moans became frantic with expectation.

Cade widened his knees behind her and put the head of his shaft against her, nudging, teasing, making her arch and squirm, trying to get him to enter her fully and end her torment. She was curled into a fetal position on her side and Trevor chose that moment to get into a better position. He pushed her bottom leg down and pulled her top one up. Then he shifted until his thick throbbing shaft was bobbing against her chin and she heard him murmur, "Suck it, Riley. That's it, baby, suck my dick while Cade fucks your ass and I eat this pussy 'til you're screaming for us."

Riley almost screamed. She had his thick shaft halfway down her throat before he had finished the first sentence. She loved the way he talked to her when they made love. It made her feel decadent and wild, with his voice deep and raspy in passion. She looked down her body and watched as he wrapped one big hand around her thigh and sank his head back in her dripping slit, pulling her closer to his face so Cade could better reach her back hole. Cade nudged closer and started slipping into her in small thrusts, deeper and deeper with each one. Riley felt only blinding passion as he filled her more and more.

Trevor lapped and sucked and took nips on her clit that were just hard enough to make her moan with each one. It was too much, she was on the edge, and it was razor sharp. She couldn't hold back any more, she started sucking deep and hard on Trevor as her body stopped obeying, and she started fighting to move. Her body simply could not hold still a moment longer, and she turned wild on them, trying to thrash and squirm.

Smack. Cade's hand was sharp on her ass. "Hold still." *Slap.* "Dammit, Riley. Ah, shit." It was Cade, slapping hard on her ass cheek, trying to keep his rhythm gentle and finding it impossible with her turning into living wildfire in their arms. Trevor bit down on her in an effort to control her too, but she was beyond the ability to stop her body. She was a creature without thought, only instinct.

Trevor growled and gripped her thighs tight, then lunged to his back, keeping her sweet pussy in his mouth and dragging her on top of him to straddle his face. Once there, he reached one hand down his body to fist in her hair and hold her head so he could fuck her hard and fast in the mouth, bumping and shoving into the back of her throat and thrilling to her efforts to suck and swallow around his ferocious rhythm.

Cade smiled in grim satisfaction. He grabbed the handful of hair from Trevor, taking over the duty of keeping her head still for them. He leaned over her to watch the furious pace Trevor had set in her mouth, thrilling to the sight of that flesh pumping in and out of her beautiful lips. He tightened his grip and shook her head back and fourth and then into the thrusts a couple of times, helping Trevor fuck her mouth. All the while, Riley moaned and sucked and tried to keep up, making it obvious that she was relishing every second of this.

"Riley. When are you going to learn?" he asked, nudging her mouth down onto Trevor's cock, feeling it bump into the back of her throat and then keeping her there for a full thirty seconds before letting her up for a breath. "If you don't hold still, you could get hurt."

Cade straddled her and plunged back into her ass from behind. Riley's whole body clenched and she cried out as an orgasm raged through her body like an eruption. He pulled back until just the head was in her and lunged again, hard. Deep. Then he pulled back and let himself go. Deep, fast, hard, riding her like he hadn't let himself in her ass before. He knew he was not going to last as he watched his shaft disappear again and again in between those perfect ass cheeks of hers. Harder, deeper.

He let go of her hair to spread her cheeks wide and changed his angle, coming in almost straight down, pushing against the walls of her pussy as he did, his balls slapping against that sweet dripping opening with each descent. Trevor was working nonstop on her clit, his arms banded around her lower back holding her arms trapped to her sides while he increased his rhythm into her mouth.

It was too much. The sights, the sensations—Cade peaked. Like a bomb centered in his groin, he exploded out of himself and into her. His shouts were loud and guttural as he rode waves that felt like they had no end.

Trevor felt it. He felt the intensity with which Cade came and it seemed to pass to him. His balls clenched and tightened and somehow he forced himself not to move, his body gripped on the edge of climax, just right there, only a stroke away and he didn't move. Holding back his climax until he could bring Riley just once more before he let go. Riley though, wasn't frozen. Instead, she seemed to be caught in a frenzy and when he stopped, she doubled her movements, sucking and tonguing his cock like her life depended on it. Trevor had no chance to hold back against her and shouted his climax into her pussy as he flooded her mouth.

The three of them shook with aftershocks as they tried to gain control of their breathing. Sweat clung and eventually cooled on their skin as they laid together, bodies touching and hands caressing in the aftermath.

"I love you." Riley was the first to break the silence, the emotions too big to keep inside after what they had just shared. Both men hugged tight to her for an endless minute. She knew they were conveying the effect of her declaration on them, knowing she was speaking to them both and knowing she meant it just as deep for them both. Riley didn't feel slighted by the lack of verbal response. She knew they would each tell her when and how they wanted, and she was okay with that.

While Trevor gently stroked patterns on her smooth belly, Cade sifted his fingers through her hair, his thoughts calm and serene for the first time since that night. The night they almost lost her. He watched how the light changed in her hair as it sifted through his fingers and let himself wallow in the serenity of having the two people he loved close and safe. All too soon, reality would invade, for now it was enough to just hold and be held.

Chapter Eighteen

That night, while Trevor and Riley went to the rec center, Cade waited in his office for Detective Brice Marshall. Cade's cousin had chosen to go into law enforcement and risk his life daily instead of relying on his trust fund. Cade, who had also felt the need to forge his own path, was one of the only family members who didn't question his choice or try and get him to resign. The family didn't begrudge him work, in fact, most of them worked in some way, but they all were horrified that he'd chosen such a dangerous profession. If he loved and believed in the law, his parents had argued, why not become a lawyer? However, Brice had no patience for the politics and legal tap-dancing that profession demanded. He much preferred police work. The rules were straightforward, and the lines between good and bad were clear and direct—if the law was broken, arrest the lawbreaker. Simple. His work was rewarding and satisfied the young boy still inside him who'd watched every cop show there ever was and dreamed of growing up to one day be the one to stop the bad guys.

"So Mom told me Aunt Kate said you're in love," Brice said by way of greeting as he walked in without knocking and made himself at home in a chair across from Cade. He had the dark hair and burnished coloring of the Marshall's but instead of Marshall-blue, his eyes were a dark brown, inherited from his mother's side of the family. His smile was teasing and reminded

Cade of younger more carefree days.

"Well, my Mom said Aunt Charlotte told her you got caught with another man's wife," Cade shot back with a grin. This was a familiar dance, one that had been performed between the two their whole lives. The mothers in this family were the grapevine. If anyone needed to know what was happening in a relative's life, all they had to do was tap either of the mothers.

"It was another man's fiancé," Brice shot back, resigned to the family's gossip chain, but still a little affronted that they thought he'd be party to breaking up a marriage. "She wasn't going to marry him anyway. I was only the means with which she made that point clear."

He didn't point out that he would not have been a party to that if he'd known she had planned for her fiancé to catch them. It made it worse that she'd used him, and he did not want that known if he could help it. It was bad enough that he had gotten involved with an engaged woman in the first place. But it was that damn hero complex of his, he reflected ruefully.

He could not resist a damsel in distress. And what a damsel. She was a knockout with red hair and big tits, and she'd clung to him and wept prettily as she'd begged him to hold her tighter and help her forget. So he had. With his tongue down her throat and his hand up her crotch he'd done some forgetting of his own too. Like forgetting that he was in another man's house, and in another man's woman. That is until that other man had shown up and all hell broke loose.

"Well, in that case..." Cade said with a mocking bow of his head. Brice grabbed the nearest thing he could reach and threw it at him with some advice on what he could do to himself. Cade laughed and caught the paperweight easily with a chuckle.

"Well, you've had my invoices for a week now. I hope to hell you were able to find more from them than I was able to."

"It's a hell of a mess you got on your hands, Cade," Brice started, all humor leaving him as he turned his attention to the file he'd brought with him. "As far as I can see, it's got to be one or all of three people..." As Brice laid out his suspicions and the paths he had taken to get to those conclusions Cade felt a chill settle in his spine. All three were people he trusted and had placed in powerful positions in his employ.

He had known it would be that way, of course he'd known that. They couldn't have had access to the invoices otherwise, but it still was a shock to see it laid out in black and white. Cade steeled himself for what came next and settled in to dissect three people he considered friends.

"Annie's on your list, Brice," Cade stated with surprise. Brice knew Annie as well as he did, and he was more than a little shocked that she would show up on the short list. "C'mon, we've known her since she was what? Six, seven years old? How could you think it would be her?"

"Yeah,—" Brice looked him cold in the eye, "—and I'm a cop who has learned all too clearly the statistics of close friends and family who commit crimes against their own." Cade shook his head as if to object, but Brice went on. "Look at the circumstances here. She was here only about a month when it started, nothing that we could find happened before she got into town. She signed for most of the deliveries and was at least on the premises for all of them. Look, I don't want to think she could do this shit any more than you do. But I wouldn't be doing you any favors if I didn't include her. The fact is she's the most likely for this, and if she wasn't practically family I would've already questioned her."

"Okay. I still think you're way off base with this, but okay. Don't roll your eyes at me, I mean it. She's been here trying to get me and Trevor to take her out. I hardly think a girl who's hot for me would be stealing from me and then try to kill me. Maybe you've been a cop too long, but attempted murder is hardly ever considered flirting out in the real world."

Brice knew that Cade felt that was a point in her favor, but to him it was just another mark against her. He remembered Annie better than he thought Cade did. He remembered a spoiled little brat who was decidedly vicious in her tantrums whenever she didn't get her way. He remembered watching her bat her eyes and prettily plead with her father for a new bike on one of his many summers there. When told no, gently but firmly, the pretty little girl had quickly turned into an ugly little demon. One who had shouted and stomped and swung at her father until, red faced, he'd had to carry her from the yard and upstairs to their apartment. Moreover, after two weeks of never seeing her without a pout and red-rimmed eyes, she was riding a brand new bike. Brice shook his head at the memory. If he had ever acted that way he doubted that he would have ever seen a bike again.

"Here's what I want to do," Brice stated and laid out a plan of action while Cade interjected with his own ideas and it was another two hours before they left the office.

As the two walked into the restaurant lobby, Brice stopped in his tracks. Every muscle in his body tensed as if he were ready for an attack and his gaze zeroed in on the cocktail lounge. Cade knew who had caught his attention before he looked. Brice had very similar tastes as he and Trevor. Riley was the only woman he knew who could stop them in their tracks.

Riley was in a particularly decadent outfit tonight. She wore a Grecian style dress in a lightweight white that swayed and ruffled around her like she created her own breeze. It hung loosely, but hugged every curve at the same time. It was slit to her navel in the front and the back draped lovingly across her luscious rear. It also left her entire back beautifully bare. A rhinestone collar around her neck was attached to the dress. She wore matching rhinestone bracelets on each wrist and her hair was piled on top of her head in a mass of curls with tiny rhinestones winking in the light from among them. When she spotted them and started walking forward they caught glimpses of her thighs thru the leg slits, that is if a man could tear his gaze away from the swaying of her breasts that were loose in that dress. Cade didn't know what she did to that garment to make it stay so stubbornly in place, and he was both glad for it and a little disgruntled.

Brice was still staring open-mouthed when Riley stopped in front of him and smiled warmly up into his face. Cade almost felt sorry for him. He remembered all too well the impact of her smile the first time he saw it. He was still reeling.

"Hi," she began and put her hand out to Brice. "I'm Riley. You must be Brice."

Brice managed to close his mouth before he drooled and clasped her hand in both of his. She was a vision with her big dark eyes and a mouth that made him want to weep that she belonged to his cousin. First the redhead now this. The world just wasn't right as far as he was concerned. He bent down to brush a kiss on her cheek, and the subtle fragrance of her perfume mixed with the essence that was pure female heat made his blood run thick. His voice was just a little too gruff when he replied, "Pleased to meet you." He shot a gaze at Cade as he said, "My cousin's a lucky guy. You're breathtaking." He was charmed when her cheeks got pink, and she nodded her thanks for the compliment.

178

"Brice. You mean to tell me you haven't gotten yourself dead yet?" Trevor said as he came up behind Riley and gave Brice a good-natured shove on his shoulder.

"Superman can't die," Brice, replied, "you know that."

"Hey, didn't you hear?" Trevor said, "Superman did die."

"I have heard that rumor. I've chosen to ignore it." Brice winked at Riley with this reply and then asked Cade, "Got time for a drink?"

The four of them headed back to the lounge with Riley in front. She could feel the intensity of their gazes on her. Riley smiled wryly to herself and thought this must be what a gazelle feels like in front of a den of lions. When she reached the rich mahogany bar, she turned her back to it and rested both elbows on it behind her, showcasing the split in her gown to its fullest. If they were going to gawk, by golly she would give 'em something to gawk at, she thought.

All three men stood frozen and transfixed. They watched as each delicate breath she took lifted and parted her gown. She could tell they were marveling that the material clung against all rules of gravity, hoping that with the next breath it would shift and reveal the flesh it so barely concealed.

"For crying out loud, fellas," Riley said in exasperation, "it's double sticky tape and it's not going to give or I wouldn't be standing here like this." She laughed softly and shook her head, but they didn't share her lighthearted manner. As one by one they lifted their gazes to meet hers she realized that what for her had been teasing, they had taken very seriously. The look of arousal was apparent on the three men's faces, and Riley quickly sobered. She was unsure what to do. Brice was an unknown element to her. He was handsome and very dashing with his cop mystique, but she was in love with two men and did not think she had the room in her heart, or body for a third.

Cade, always in tune to her every expression, leaned in to whisper in her ear, "We don't share. Rest assured that Trevor and I are the last men who will ever touch you."

"Although, "Trevor cut in, "Brice always makes a wonderful audience."

He quickly explained to her that a year or so ago, they'd had a particularly adventurous girlfriend when they had invited Brice over for dinner. Half way thru the meal, she had stood up from the table and taken off her dress. While he'd politely refused the offer she made to join them, he had stayed and observed. That evening had been a satisfying surprise for all of them and it had been repeated on a few equally satisfying evenings since.

Riley looked again at Brice. He was handsome, tall, well built from the way his clothes fit, but it was his eyes that caught her. There was an intensity there that caused her to shiver in appreciation. There was also kindness there, maybe it was the cop in him, or maybe it was just his nature, but there was something in him that just oozed trustworthiness and honor. He did not fit the image she had in her mind of what a voyeur would look like. He definitely seemed a hands-on kind of guy. When she said as much, he replied, "Oh, believe me. If this were a situation where I was allowed a hands-on approach with you, I'd take you so thoroughly you'd forget these two and run away with me."

He smiled in a way that could only be described as cocky and added, "But there is a thrill that can be had as an observer that can't be achieved anywhere else. Tell me, have you ever gotten hot watching a skin flick or reading a steamy novel?" When she shyly nodded he said, "There you have it. Only take that feeling and multiply it by a hundred when the sex you're watching is in person."

"Oh," Riley whispered.

Twenty minutes later Riley thought she was going to go mad. Brice had directed the men to undress her as soon as she had gotten to the living room. He had then instructed her to lay back in one of Cade's black leather chairs. After she'd sat he had Trevor drape her legs over the armrests, he then told him to pull her arms back over the top of the chair and told her not to move them for any reason. Then he'd told Cade to go down on her while Trevor kissed her and played with her breasts. He'd sat quiet and watchful as the men had devastated her and in ten mind-blowing minutes she'd been screaming into Trevor's mouth as Cade had relentlessly sucked and licked and kissed her to climax.

"Cade," Brice's voice penetrated the fog that engulfed her mind. "Step to the side of the chair and let me see you make her gush." Cade gave a last suckling, swirling kiss to her clit and moved behind the arm of the chair.

Riley knew what was coming. They had done this to her a handful of times. It was devastating every time. It was the most explosive, earth shattering experience she'd ever had. They gave it to her sparingly, like a decadent dessert reserved for special occasions and Riley whimpered, her body quivering in anticipation. With Cade out of the way, Brice had a clear view of her open, dripping sheath, his gaze was zeroed in on it and Riley felt connected to him in this incredible act of intimacy.

"Trevor," Brice said without looking up. "Let Riley suck on you while Cade brings her." Trevor stood with a murmured, "My pleasure." Trevor's long fingered hand brushed her cheek and turned her face to him after he had shed his clothes, easing the bulbous head of his shaft between her lips. Both of them hummed in pleasure as he slid to the back of her throat. He then slid that hand down and gently but firmly clasped her neck, only slightly restricting her breathing. His other hand grasped a handful of her hair, effectively holding her face a willing prisoner to his thrusts.

Then Cade slid his wide hand between her legs. Her gaze was locked on Trevor's when Cade dipped two strong fingers into her and curled them up. Trevor slid slowly in to the back of her mouth, and Cade flexed twice. Riley jumped and a moan sounded in her chest.

"Hold still." The command came from Cade and the heel of his other hand settled firmly just above her mound. Then he flexed again. Riley's legs started to close, and her arms came down. "Stop," Trevor said, giving a sharp yank to her hair. "You know better, little one." He gave a couple quick short thrusts into her mouth, and Riley watched as his muscles bunched and passion tightened his features. Cade flexed again, hard and fast, and Riley lost her ability to think.

Brice could smell her. It was intoxicating, she smelled as good as she looked, and she looked like nirvana. He watched as, against the men's warnings, she started to buck and Cade put more pressure on her with his free hand and doubled the pace of his thrusts. Brice swore soft and low when Riley screamed and a fountain flushed from her body to spray her thighs and splash back on her stomach as Cade continued to pump her. Cade leaned over her with a groan and furiously sucked on her clit, clamping his hands on her thighs to keep them open when she screamed again and started to fight their hold on her. It was an amazing thing to watch, and Brice felt waves of heat and lust pouring off the trio as they strained and bucked together.

Cade stood and stripped his clothes off without waiting for

direction from Brice, his focus on Trevor as he fucked fast and deep in her mouth while her body continued to twitch with aftershocks. "Fuck her in the chair, Trev," Brice said, his voice sex-roughened and deep. Trevor stepped back and lifted her as if she weighed nothing then sat on the chair. He pulled her onto his lap backward, so her sweet ass was nestled on his lap while he faced Brice and plunged into her throbbing sheath. "Put your feet on his thighs Riley...yeah, like that. No, keep your knees wide. Umm, that's good. Pretty." Trevor's hands cupped her bottom and he set up a hard fast rhythm that brought more screams of delight from her. Cade stepped up and kissed her deep, his tongue thrusting as fast between her lips as Trevor's shaft between her legs. He groaned and pulled her head back by the hair, sliding his fingers between those lips now and watching as she licked and sucked while he slid them to the back of her throat. Then it was his shaft slipping and sliding along her tongue, his groans mixing with theirs. They both took her with a pounding pace that made it impossible to last.

All too soon, Cade recognized the signs that Trevor was at his limit, his rhythm breaking as he started to lose control. Cade changed his angle and started thrusting faster into her mouth, determined that they would reach the end together. Trevor pulled back on Riley's ass and his next thrust hit her g-spot. Riley detonated and gushed again. It was a surprise to all of them and the sight of her orgasm spraying from her body like a faucet galvanized the men.

Trevor shouted and pumped so hard into her it lifted them off the chair as his climax joined hers and then Cade joined them, his semen filling and spilling from her frantically sucking mouth.

Brice groaned as his body gave an involuntary thrust and it took every bit of his will power to prevent himself from doing some flooding of his own.

Brice didn't dare move. He was so hard he thought even his slacks brushing against his aching shaft would be enough to bring him. He had seen Cade and Trevor with two other women. Women they had cared for and been passionate about, but it was nothing compared to what he had just witnessed.

The look that had been on Cade's face as he came into her mouth had been more than lust. He had looked into her eyes and in that moment had been vulnerable and stark. He really is in love with her, Brice thought, they both were.

As his body reluctantly subsided, he mused that even though theirs wasn't a conventional relationship, it was a genuine one and wondered how all the families concerned were going to handle the trio. It was certainly going to be interesting come next Christmas he thought and quietly made his way to the guest room he used whenever he stayed over.

Chapter Nineteen

The next morning Riley was a mess of nerves and anxiety. They were leaving for the airport in three hours to see her parents. She was a complete wreck. She knew that they loved her and wanted what was best for her, but what if they couldn't see that Cade and Trevor were what *was* best for her? What was she going to do if her father looked at her as if she had disappointed him? She didn't think she would be able to face it if it came down to a choice between her parents and her men. The only thing she could do was wait, hope and pray that it never came to that.

In the meantime she would cook. It was the only thing that calmed her nerves. She would make her dad's favorite cookies to bring him, and then maybe a batch for the employee's downstairs too. She shook her head at herself as she sifted flour into a bowl, she sure hoped the flight wasn't delayed, if it was she was going to need more flour.

Riley looked up with a puzzled frown when she heard the elevator sound. The guys had left only twenty minutes ago. Trevor to see to some things at the rec center, and Cade to his broker's office, something he'd said about contracts before he left. She was a little puzzled when she saw Ann step into the foyer.

"Hello, Ann," Riley said, remembering not to use her

nickname at the last second. "Umm...you just missed the guys. They had some errands to run before we leave."

"I know," Ann replied with a sneer. "I waited all morning for them to go. I need to talk to you alone." Ann had thought and stewed for a week about what to do. She knew that Cade was onto her stealing. She didn't think that he knew it was her yet, but she was desperate.

Her only hope was to get rid of Riley and switch their attention to her. Obviously the little tramp was boring them, or Cade would not have dug into the missing items. Well, she would make sure they were kept busy once this little slut was gone. She would cloud their minds with sex. Then beg them to take her on a trip across Europe. By the time they got back, the little discrepancies in the inventory would be a distant memory, and her troubles would be behind her.

She would not have needed to steal from him if he had only started dating her when she first came here. It was his fault. If he had followed her plan she wouldn't be in this fix and wouldn't have to be here doing this. Well, there was no hope for it. What's done was done. She had to follow this through and then it would be easy street from here on out.

Riley wiped her hands off and gestured to Ann to sit. "If you want to talk, let's have a seat. Can I get you a drink? Some juice or tea?" Riley felt tension coil in her stomach as Ann just stood in the middle of the living room and looked around. It was as if she were taking inventory or something, and it made Riley nervous.

"Look, I want you out of here. I'm prepared to offer you twenty thousand dollars to disappear. Pack up your shit and leave, and I will write you a check."

Riley was stunned. "What are you talking about? What on earth makes you think I would take your money? For that matter, why would you think I'd leave?" Anger was boiling in her gut and her voice shook with the force it took to keep quiet. Ann might think they were alone but that was because she didn't know Brice had spent the night, and Riley did not want to wake him. Whatever it was that Ann was doing was between her and Ann. She didn't want to drag anyone else into this ugliness.

"What I think is that you are a money hungry little whore who saw dollar signs the first time they laid eyes on you. I'm offering you way more than you'll get from them once they tire of you." She shook her short blonde hair back from her face and paced closer to Riley as she went on. "C'mon, Riley. We're both girls here. You don't have to act for me. I know what they do to you. I know you must hate it. But hey? Who could blame you really, when you look at this place? And the clothes they're showing you off in? What about those rocks in your ears? You get those for taking it up the ass like a good little slut?

"You're only here for the money. Why else would you be here? I'm offering you it all up front. Believe me it's more than they'll give you when they're done with you." She was face to face with Riley. "They will be done with you, Riley. No matter what lies they've told you to make you believe otherwise. They will be done with you and throw you away like the used up condom you are, and then where will you be?" She stepped back, took her checkbook out of her purse and arched one perfectly tweezed brow at her. "Twenty thousand to walk away now, before they've grown bored with you. Look at it this way, you can live out the rest of your life being the one that got away instead of just one of the many who was tossed back."

Brice sucked in his breath and clenched his fists. So angry

187

that he could easily picture himself snapping her vicious little neck. But he stayed out of sight, hoping she would say more to incriminate herself.

Riley was not a fighter, she never had been and had never even hit anyone in her life. But right now, she wanted to hit Ann so bad it was making her arms shake with the effort it took to hold back.

"If you don't leave *now* I'm going to call security and have them drag you out by your hair."

"Oh. Come. On. Is that all you've got? Security? You spineless little nobody. Don't you get it? You don't belong here. I do. I know everyone down there and if you call them, you'll be the one who is dragged out by your hair, after I tell them how I caught you with the man I saw you sneak in here the minute Cade and Trevor left. You know, the same one who ran out half naked when I charged up here to see what you were up to." While Riley stared at her in open-mouthed shock, Ann shook her head and continued.

"Get out now, Riley, before I have to get ugly. Just take the check and don't look back." She ripped the check from her book and stuffed it in Riley's cleavage with a sneer. Her sneer turned to resignation when Riley tore the check into pieces and threw them in her face.

"Get out now. You may be able to convince security for a little while, but Cade and Trevor would never believe you. Now leave."

"You know, I'm almost glad you did that. I worked hard for that money and was not happy about giving it to you. Nevertheless, I wanted to give you a fair chance. After all, I felt kind of bad about the whole near death thing. I mean, you were supposed to die, I gave you enough to kill a buffalo, but after, when you pulled through I thought that maybe I was going too far. But now I see that you deserved it. Just like you deserve this."

Ann moved before Riley could react. She pulled a gun from her purse and a dart shot into her gut that felt like the sting of a scorpion.

Brice registered what he heard a second too late and stepped from around the corner to see Riley clasp her stomach and crumble to the floor.

"Freeze," he shouted. He didn't have his gun, but experience had shown him that a commanding tone was enough to bluff most crooks. "Drop the gun and get on the floor. Now." Ann startled when she heard him and cursed under her breath.

"What the fuck are you doing here? You are going to ruin everything." Her voice was the same shrill whine that he remembered. Brice wondered how she'd hidden her true self from Cade for the whole year of working with him. He walked to her, thinking that it was a shame that it had turned out to be her after all. They had watched her grow up, and he liked her folks, this was gonna kill them.

He should have been paying attention. He had been distracted and had underestimated her because he knew her. He never checked to make sure she'd dropped the gun, didn't think she'd gone so far over the edge that she would turn and shoot him even if she hadn't. But she did, and she smiled like a damn cat when he staggered to his knees as he fumbled to remove the dart from his chest.

Chapter Twenty

Mike was scared. He liked this new job and he needed it. Three years ago, his dad had died of a heart attack and left his mom with four kids to support and a lot of debt to be paid off. Mike had quit college and come back home to try to keep his family together. His mom was an immigrant who had never worked outside the home. He knew his mom being there for him and his brothers and sister was the reason none of them were ever in trouble. So as long as he was living, his mother was going to stay at home. His three younger siblings were too young—the oldest was only thirteen, not old enough yet to help with the bills. So it was up to him.

This job was his ticket. It paid better than what his father had made, and with the overtime the boss let him work, things were looking good. He had not known how much his schooling was pinching his dad. The debt it had racked up made Mike cringe every time he thought about it. Well, he was taking care of it and if things kept up at the same pace, he'd have the biggest credit card paid off in six months. The rest would be paid off in just a year and a half after that.

But only if he kept this job. There was a buzz going around about someone stealing, and they were looking at him for it. He guessed he couldn't blame them for thinking it. He was the newest, and his money problems were no secret, but it still made his gut burn to be looked at as a thief.

Especially when he knew who the thief was. Since saving every penny was all he could think about, he often walked to work instead of taking the subway or a cab. The walk took him by some rough neighborhoods and about a month ago, he'd seen Annie the scarecrow bitch along the way.

At first, he hadn't thought about it. Figured she was making a crack deal since she was meeting with some pretty shady characters. It made sense considering she was skinny as a crack ho, but as he'd passed he saw them hand her money, not the other way around. It was peculiar enough that he'd looked back as he passed. He saw her open the trunk of her car and the thugs with her had started unloading boxes. Sure, it didn't prove that she was the one stealing, but it was proof enough for him. His only problem was that he didn't know how to get them to look at her without making himself look even guiltier by pointing fingers.

Mike was worrying over the dilemma while cleaning the storage room when he saw Ann let those same thugs in the back door. The place was closed this early, and there wasn't supposed to be anybody here. He was only here because the boss had okayed some more overtime for him again. Mike wasted no time and headed for the closest phone once they had gotten onto the elevator; this was his chance. If they caught her red-handed, he would be in the clear and his family would be too.

"Hey, Boss," Mike said when Cade answered, "I hate to bother you but I just thought there was something you should know..."

Cade had never been so scared in his life. When the call came through, he'd almost let it go to voice mail, but when he saw that it was his private line from his office phone, he'd picked up. What he heard next made his blood run cold. He'd told Mike to call 911 and had run out of his broker's office without saying a word to him. As he ran, knowing it was faster than the waiting cab, he called Trevor. He said only what was needed to get the message across, "It's Annie and she's at the penthouse with Riley." Then he hung up and sprinted as if the hounds of hell were on his heels.

Chapter Twenty-One

Ann was sweating. This was the tricky part. Security was out front. She didn't know if they ever checked the back, there was no need during the day to look in the alley was there? Well, all her boys had to do was clear out the penthouse and take the bitch with them. These guys had been buying from her for years. Cade wasn't the only one she'd lifted items from whenever things got tight. This was different though, this time she was selling a girl to them. They knew a lot of people, people who moved in that elusive and mysterious black market that everyone talked about. The part that surprised her was the gang hadn't even blinked when she'd asked them if they knew someone who'd like a girl who was into gangbangs. They'd named an enormous price if she could deliver. Since the fat little tramp had refused to cooperate, she'd called them in. They were going to take a bunch of things from the house and make it look like Riley had stolen them and then split. No one would ever see her again. Simple.

The big problem now was what to do with Brice. They didn't want a man. They offered to kill him for her, but the price of that was going to be everything that they had been going to pay her for Riley. Moreover, murdering a man she had known since childhood was turning out to be a lot harder than she would've thought it to be. Nevertheless, she could not let him live. He'd been there and seen her, and she couldn't think of any way out of this unless Brice disappeared.

"Go ahead then. Take care of him. Just make it quick, before he wakes up, at least he won't feel anything."

She walked toward the living room when she saw one of the two men pull out a gun. She was not going to watch, she couldn't. Nothing surprised her more than to see the elevator open and Cade rushing in with cops behind him.

"No." Ann was so angry and frustrated she couldn't see straight. It was finished, done. All her plans and plotting, all she had been through for the last year, all for nothing. As anger pumped through her veins like a super drug, she raced to where they had plopped Riley's body with the junk they were going to take. She didn't know what she would have done once she got to her, tear her apart with her bare hands probably. But she never got the chance. Cade rushed her and fisted one hand in her hair, the other around one of her arms and yanked her off her feet. Her howls of rage reverberated through the penthouse as he tossed her on the couch as if she weighed less than the throw pillows she landed on. Then he stood towering over her like an avenging angel.

"You stupid son of a bitch. What are you doing here? You ruined everything. I hate you! I hate you!" she screamed as she kicked out at him and her arms pounded into the cushions. The tantrum not unlike the many she had been throwing her whole life.

Cade could not believe the sight before him. Annie was flailing like a spoiled two-year-old, and he thought that she just might have lost her mind. When Trevor rushed in, he watched him take in the whole scene in a glance—the shouting cops who were cuffing the two thugs, the trashed apartment and Annie cursing and thrashing on the couch. The two locked gazes across the room, and they shared very similar thoughts of astonishment and gratitude that they hadn't taken her out after all. Relief that they had dodged this particular bullet.

Then as one, they turned when Riley moaned and tried to push herself up. Some art and other things from around the penthouse surrounded her and it was clear to both of them that she was drugged. Cade reached her first and scooped her up before she tried to stand. Trevor was right behind him and the two of them crooned to her as she looked around, clearly confused.

"It's okay, Riley," Cade murmured. "God I was so scared. We were both so scared." Then he said those familiar words in her ear, "You're safe now. You're safe."

"Maybe I should go back home." Riley was still shaking late into that night. She was seated on the couch between Trevor and Cade, Brice was on a chair brooding into a cup of coffee. It had taken hours to deal with the police statements and paperwork. They were exhausted and wrung out. Ann had been charged with attempted murder, grand larceny, assaulting an officer and a slew of other crimes that Riley couldn't remember. The men she was with had been charged with more of the same. Riley couldn't get the vicious words that Ann had said out of her head. What if she was telling the truth? What if she was just here until her novelty wore off? Would the guys send her packing without a backward glance? Even with the money they were lavishing on her, did it really mean the same to them that it did to her since they had so much of it? And, neither of them had said they loved her. After the intimacies they had shared, they had never felt compelled to give her the words. She let herself believe that they would when the time was right for them. But what if the truth was that they hadn't because they didn't and it was as simple as that?

195

Brice looked up from the cup of coffee in his hand and watched his cousin and his friend's reaction to the statement. They both looked ready to murder. Before either of them could say something that would make matters worse, he spoke up.

"Don't go flying off the handle. You guys didn't hear what that bitch said to her. You gotta know she's gonna be freaked about this now."

"It doesn't matter what that cunt said," Cade spoke without taking his eyes off Riley's face. "She is a certifiable lunatic and anything she said should have no bearing whatsoever."

"She told Riley that she was just another woman in a long line, and she was fooling herself if she believed otherwise."

Trevor harrumphed in the back of his throat. "Riley would never fall for that. She knows how we feel. Don't you, little one?" When her eyes filled with tears, he was baffled and dismayed. "Riley?" he asked, voice soft and coaxing, "Ry, we love you. We both do. How can you doubt it after everything that's gone on between us?"

"Yes," Cade demanded, "how?"

"Well," Riley sniffled, voice quavering as she tried to keep it together, "you guys have never said it. We have only been together for a couple weeks, and the way she said it made it sound so stupid that I would believe this could last." She looked between the two of them, pleading for them to understand. "I mean, c'mon, as much as this feels real and as much as I want it to be forever... how can it be?"

Cade took both her hand and Trevor's, clasping them in Riley's lap. "It can because it is." He got down on his knees facing her. Trevor, in sync with him as always, followed suit. "What we have is real, and it will last. I love you, Riley. We both have loved you from the first day. Maybe we should have told you before, but we're telling you now, and we'll keep telling you until the day we die."

In the end it was Brice who convinced her. He told Riley about the other women in their lives, and how he'd known that she was different after only five minutes in her company. He spoke with such an open honesty that there just wasn't room left to doubt. Besides, he was just telling her what her heart had been saying from the first morning waking up with the two of them wrapped tight around her, she was in love and it was real.

Epilogue

Six months later Riley was getting married. She stood in front of a mirror, looked at herself in her Vera Wang wedding gown, and tried not to cry. It had taken a professional hair and make-up crew two hours to get her looking like this. She was not about to cry and ruin their hard work before the wedding pictures were done. The dress was a vision in ivory with sequins and pearls, long flowing train and a decadently low-cut back with three chains of real diamonds swooping from shoulder to shoulder.

"Oh dear! You look like I always dreamed you would!" Riley smiled at her mom and warned, "Suck it up, Ma, if you cry, I cry. I am not going to until the pictures are done." She wrapped her arms around her mother and hugged tight.

"You're right. It would be a pity if you ruined your make-up. You look beautiful." She pulled herself together and took her daughter's hands. "Now, I know I don't have to ask, I've never seen you happier, but a mother should always ask. Are you sure this is what you want?"

Riley smiled, kissed her mother's cheek and picked up her bouquet. "This is more than I wanted. More than I dreamed was even possible, and I'm going to be happy for the rest of my life."

"Are you ready, princess?" Riley's dad was there, in his Hugo Boss tuxedo and pride gleaming from his eyes. He too, looked on the verge of tears. Riley hoped that her mascara was waterproof because she gave up the fight and let the tears fall.

It had taken her parents a while to warm up to her men. Trevor and Cade had flown them in after the fiasco with Ann and put them up in the townhouse for a month. At first her father had been aloof and her mother downright snippy. But the guys wouldn't be deterred and had systematically broken down their reserves. In the end it was the way they treated Riley that had won her parents over. It was obvious to anyone who spent more than an hour in their company that they were crazy about her and she them. Her parents had to concede that as long as they continued to treat her the way they were the three had their blessings.

"Oh. Honey." They looked over as Cade's mother came into the room. "Don't you look amazing." Riley held out a hand to her. Cade and Trevor's families had taken to her instantly, having long ago adjusted to the boys' lifestyle. They knew that for them this was indeed a lifelong commitment and couldn't be happier in the choice their sons had made.

As for the legal stuff, that was handled already. After Brice had told the guys what he'd overheard, the men had been livid. They had also wanted to make sure that there wasn't a doubt in anyone's mind about what Riley's place was in their lives. Especially hers. Each of them was now the beneficiary of the others. They had living wills that gave each other the rights and responsibilities that any spouse would have. Riley was even taking their names. She was now Riley Wellington-Marshall. Any children that they had would take the name of their biological father, and both of the men wanted children. When that time came, they would take measures to assure that they knew who was whose and that there wouldn't be room for doubt or insecurities. The ceremony today was the culmination of what they had put in place. A public declaration of devotion for all who knew them to see.

"I'm ready, Dad." Riley absolutely glowed as she spoke

those words, meaning them with every fiber of her being.

Her father led her out to the gardens where flickering candles lined the path to the two handsomest men she had ever seen. They waited side by side in identical Valentino tuxedos, ready to make a vow before their entire families that they were taking her and only her to be their wife. 'Til death do they part. The ceremony would not be a legally binding one, but it would be binding nonetheless to them.

That was all that mattered.

About the Author

Lainey lives in Lake Stevens, Washington with her husband, daughter, four cats, a dog, a fish and a bird. Lainey has dreamed of being a writer as far back as she can remember. Even when she dreamed of being an actress, in her dreams she was always starring in movies she wrote.

The racy content of this book was a sticking point for her, she had originally set out to write a romance without sex scenes. Lainey quickly became frustrated. It was just not possible for her to create the level of passion and intimacy she wanted for her characters without the love scenes. So, Lainey, with the encouragement of her mother, gave in and decided to write without her steam filter on and see where it led. Lainey was more than a little shocked, and a whole lot pleased with the end result and hopes that the readers will be too.

To learn more about Lainey, please visit www.laineyreese.com. Send an email to Lainey at lainey@laineyreese.com.

Three men, a tomboy...
and one erotic game that could change everything.

Three for Me?
© *2009 R. G. Alexander*

Simon, Eric, Rafael, Lee...and Charli. It's never mattered that Charli is the only girl in the crowd. She's always been a tomboy, anyway. Just one of the guys.

Between work and Couch Potato Thursdays, life is pretty full. Sure, no man alive can get through the friend gauntlet, but thanks to her boys and her toys, she's got plenty of fantasy material. It's a win-win situation. Until Lee has a destination wedding in Cozumel—and Charli's "best man" duties take a kinky turn.

Through what looks to be foul play by Lee's new brides, Charli finds herself on a decidedly decadent shore excursion, playing "The Race Erotic". With each sexy challenge, it becomes clearer that down deep, she desires not one, not two, but all three of her remaining single buddies.

They're the only family she's ever known. She can't imagine living without them. Will she have to choose? Or will the final score be three to one?

Warning: Naughty costumes, kinky toys, a boy, a girl...two more boys, all doing unspeakably dirty things to each other.

Available now in ebook from Samhain Publishing.

Enjoy the following excerpt from Three for Me?...

"I wanted that outfit." Natalie glared at her, looking intimidating in a leopard print body stocking.

"I'm sorry?"

Shelly came and got between them. "Nat, you know you don't get to choose your outfits. Besides, you've already been the naughty schoolgirl several times now. Give someone else a chance."

Naughty schoolgirl. Charli covered her face with her hands, peeking at herself in the mirror through her spread fingers. She'd had her hair put in pigtails. She hadn't worn pigtails since she was nine.

The little Mary Janes and thigh-high white stockings were bad enough. The plaid skirt was so short she could see her clingy white underwear that had, thankfully, been in a store-bought package beside the ensemble. But it was the shirt, most of all that was giving her fits.

Button-down and white, it stopped right beneath her breasts, leaving her midriff bare. Already so thin they could see the shadow of her areoles. Shelly and the other woman had patted her with a damp cloth, making it entirely see through. She'd never be able to face the boys again.

"Don't be nervous. It's just two songs. And it's pretty dark in there. The game rents the upstairs club for as long as we're here, so no one but the other racers will see you dance. And I'm pretty sure they'll be too busy to look."

Charli was feeling a little warm. Maybe it was from the tequila, but she wasn't necessarily afraid of this challenge. She was the lifelong friend of four very manly men. She'd been to a strip club before. And she did love to dance. If only she didn't have to wear this humiliating outfit.

She remembered what Connie had said about her having the body of a pole dancer. Had she known this would be one of the challenges? She was going to have a good long chat with Lee's new wife when they got back.

Shelly led them all to a curtained doorway. "Up those stairs you'll find a main stage that will lead you to your individual walkways. Dance one entire song on that walkway for your men. When the next song starts, give him the lap dance of his dreams, and just be open to the pleasure. It's a wonderful experience. The men know what they have to do to get the next clue, so go on and show them what you've got!"

Shelly stopped Charli as the others went on ahead. "Your guys have already been told, but I wanted to let you know that you can only pick one to lap dance with, and the other men can watch, but they aren't allowed to touch you until the song ends. Okay? Great!"

She rushed off, clipboard in hand while Charli took a deep breath. Was she really going to do this? The music started, and she walked out onto the main stage. Of course she was. She never backed down from a bet.

Charli strode to the rhythm of the beat, watching her counterparts do the Time with a smile. Dawn, despite her shyness, seemed determined to do this for Tim. And from the expression on his face, Charli could tell he appreciated it. She walked to the end of her walkway and placed her hands on her hips. "If any of you laugh at me, I'll give you a wedgie. Or steal your lunch money."

"Charli?"

"Dear God. And thank you. Amen."

"Fuck, Chuck. You look—"

She lifted her chin threateningly, but Simon's gaze was focused entirely on her breasts. He sighed. "Amazing."

"Yeah?" She caught Shelly making a dancing motion and started to sway to the music. Eric, Raf and Simon were staring at her, looking dazed and totally enthralled. Heat pooled between her thighs. Being the focus of this kind of attention felt...well it felt great. Empowering. Something she could definitely get used to.

There was a pole, and Charli had always wanted to try one. All those mountain-climbing muscles were put to good use as she leapt up onto the steel cylinder, using her thighs to cling, her arms spread out in a backward arch that gave her the perfect, upside-down view of her audience.

"Sweet Jesus."

"Did you know she could do that?"

Simon didn't respond, barely took his blue eyes off her long enough to blink.

Charli's smile was wicked. She lifted herself up, sliding down the pole until she was on her knees on her walkway, crawling closer to the edge of the stage. "How are the others doing? Are we winning?"

"Who knows? Who cares?" Eric's cheeks were flushed, and Rafael looked over at him, before turning his attention back to Charli.

"I forgot. You're fulfilling Professor Eric's favorite fantasy, sugar. He's gonna have a hard time keeping his hands off you."

Charli stopped her forward motion, sitting up to rub her hands slowly over her damp shirt. Her nipples were hard. Sensitive. The three heartfelt groans made her chuckle. "What fantasy?"

"Nothing." Eric glared at Rafael, but Raf just smiled.

"No use lying about it, friend. Eric used to tell us that his favorite fantasy was of you as one of his students. One of his bad students. Who needed to be punished."

Charli blinked. The gush of arousal dampened her white schoolgirl panties, and she slid her hand between her legs unconsciously.

"She likes that idea, Eric." Simon's voice was rough, and she shivered as though he'd touched her skin. "She *really* likes it. Don't you, Chuck?"

She stuck out her tongue, but inside she was quaking. Images of her bent over Eric's desk, being spanked, being fucked, filled her mind. She closed her eyes, arching her neck as her hand disappeared beneath her skirt.

The music ended and Rafael made a sound of frustration. All three men shifted in their seats.

"Time for the next round, ladies. You know what to do. You too, guys." Shelly's perky voice jerked Charli out of her fantasy, making her blush. The new music was slower, sultrier. Reminded her of sex. As if anything didn't right now.

"You have to pick one, babe. Have to pick one of us to dance for."

It wasn't as difficult a choice as she thought. She'd been planning to pick him anyway, if only because she'd thought he was the least likely to tease her. But now. Now she wanted to choose him for an entirely different reason.

"I choose Eric."

LaVergne, TN USA
25 January 2011
213966LV00002B/6/P